HOBBS AND THE KID

Other books by John M. Sharpe

One Step From Hell

HOBBS AND
THE KID

•

John M. Sharpe

COPY 1

AVALON BOOKS
NEW YORK

Published by Avalon Books,
an imprint of Thomas Bouregy & Co., Inc.
New York, NY

Library of Congress Cataloging-in-Publication Data

Sharpe, John M.
    Hobbs and the kid / John M. Sharpe.
        p.   cm.
    ISBN 978-0-8034-7465-9 (hardcover : acid-free paper)
    I. Title.
    PS3619.H3566H63 2012
    813'.6—dc23

                                        2011033933

PRINTED IN THE UNITED STATES OF AMERICA
ON ACID-FREE PAPER
BY RR DONNELLEY, HARRISONBURG, VIRGINIA

Chapter One

"How come we don't git to fight the Apaches, Sarge?" Levi Haines asked. His smooth black face was drawn into a frown and glistened with sweat in the Arizona heat as he struggled to match his sergeant's long strides.

"Because we're assigned here as scouts, Corporal." Sergeant Daniel Hobbs clomped along the wooden sidewalk that led away from the company commander's office. "You heard the cap'n. Right now our job's to find Geronimo, not fight him."

"I bet if we was white," Levi persisted, "they'd let us take on them Indians."

"You'll get your chance to die soon enough," Hobbs replied.

Levi's eyes widened for a moment, showing more white than usual; then he said, "Yeah, but don't it bother ya, Sarge, not gettin' to fight?"

"Sure, it bothers me. That's why I put in for a transfer."

"A transfer," Levi repeated, just as they reached Hobbs' quarters. "Where?"

"An outfit up north." Hobbs opened the rough plank door and paused. "Fall the men out. Field packs, weapons, thirty rounds of rifle ammunition per man, rations for ten days." Then, ignoring Levi's questioning look, he stepped into the dark opening to his quarters.

1

The room felt cool compared to the searing heat outside. Hobbs began taking pieces of equipment down from the pegs wedged into the adobe walls: a cloth-covered water canteen, a leather belt with cartridge pouch and holster, and a sheathed bowie knife. He withdrew the single-action army Colt, checked the cylinder for load, then, with a resounding smack that was loud in the small room, thrust the weapon back into the holster.

He strapped on the gun belt and, with no wasted motion, stripped a blanket from one of the narrow bunks in a corner of the room. With a skill born of years of practice he rolled the blanket into a tight cylinder and secured it with two leather thongs. Then Hobbs exchanged his small, peaked garrison cap for a sandy-colored campaign hat with a broad brim turned up in front and a crown stained by years of sweat. He went to a crude stand against one wall and checked his reflection in the jagged sliver of smoky mirror hanging over the tin washbasin.

The black eyes peering back at him seemed accusing. *Maybe Levi's right,* Hobbs said to himself. *It ain't proper we don't get to fight. I know what Cap'n Horner said, but we're the best doggone soldiers in the U.S. Cavalry. I didn't join the buffalo soldiers to shovel horse dung and let the white troopers do all the fightin'.* Then he squared his shoulders, adjusted the campaign hat low across his forehead, and scowled at the mirror. "Forget it, Hobbs," he said to the image looking back at him. "You're a soldier. Act like it."

After a quick look around the room he grabbed the .38-55 Winchester from its rack by the door and strode back out into the glare of the summer afternoon. Outside, astride a stout army pony, Levi waited at the head of a column of ten mounted riders, all dressed in cavalry blue. Under fresh, near-white campaign hats their black faces shone in the desert heat. The man directly behind Levi held a guidon, the flag emblazoned with the insignia of the Ninth Cavalry Regiment. Hobbs walked to where Levi held a waiting mount and rammed the rifle home into its scabbard, secured his bedroll, then took the reins and swung easily up into the saddle.

He glanced at his corporal, "Ready?"

Levi nodded, and they turned their horses, and Hobbs raised one hand. "Column of twos—forward—ho!" The troopers wheeled into position and started across the parade square, a small billow of dust rising in their wake.

Hobbs felt a swelling pride as he led his squad through the sandy enclosure, past the twenty-foot pole in the center of the square where the Stars and Stripes hung limp in the merciless heat. As they moved slowly toward the open gate in the high adobe walls, they passed an assortment of civilians and soldiers, nearly all white but with an occasional black or Mexican scattered among them. Hobbs was aware of each glance from the bystanders, and he sat a little straighter in his saddle as he enjoyed the admiring looks on some of the upturned faces.

The squad passed a row of squat buildings that housed the sutler store and the officers' quarters. As they came abreast of the commanding officer's doorway, Captain Horner came out onto the wooden porch, leaned against a support post, and lit his pipe. He watched the passing troopers through a cloud of smoke.

"Eyes right!" Hobbs barked, and he rendered a crisp salute.

Horner took the pipe from his mouth, straightened to attention, and returned Hobbs' salute. *He's a first-rate officer,* Hobbs thought, as he stared into the other man's cold blue

eyes, *even if I don't always like what he says. He's tough
but fair, and ya can't ask for more than that.*

His mind drifted back to the conversation of two hours
before in Horner's office. The captain tapped on the territorial map hanging on one wall. "After Cochise died in '74,"
he said, "the U.S. Government forced about four thousand
Apache onto a reservation." He pointed with his pipe. "Here,
at San Carlos.

"Things were fairly peaceful while General Crook was
Territorial Commander. But the officers who came after
him . . ." Horner paused, as if giving careful thought to
his next words. "Well," he said at last, "let's just say, it didn't
work out. Some of the Apache got homesick. Others wanted
to keep raiding into Mexico. And the Lord knows none of
them had enough to eat. So a few of the tribal chiefs like
Victorio and Nana started leading raids off the reservation.
But now things have really gone to pot."

"Geronimo?" Hobbs volunteered.

Horner nodded. "And a young buck named Sanchez. He's
wild and hotheaded. Some think he's about ready to challenge Geronimo for leadership of the tribe."

"I've heard of him," Hobbs said.

Horner motioned to another section of the map. "I want
you to take your squad and scout this area." He tapped the
new location with his pipe. "Near the Dragoon Mountains,
Cochise's old stronghold. See if you can locate Geronimo's
camp. If you do, get word back to me as fast as you can." He
paused and fixed Hobbs with a firm look. "But your job is
to find Geronimo, Sergeant, not engage him. Got that?"

Hobbs had tried to argue that he and his men were eager
to fight, but Horner would have none of it. "We've been all
over this before, Sergeant," he insisted. "That'll be all."

The memory of the stinging words jarred Hobbs out of his reverie. "Eyes front!" he snapped as he passed out of Horner's line of sight. Then he adjusted his hat again and spurred his horse into an easy lope. The squad followed suit, and with the clank of equipment and the squeak of leather they moved through the gate toward the barren, rolling landscape. Hobbs looked back at his men, all riding stiffly and proudly as they passed out of the fort, under a plank with the words FORT HUACHUCA, ARIZONA TERR. burned into it.

Levi moved to Hobbs' side. "Who is this Geronimo, Sarge?"

"Chief of the Chiricahua tribe. He took over after Cochise died."

Levi smiled, his eyes filled with a mixture of excitement and curiosity. "What's he like?"

"He's got more guts than an army mule," Hobbs answered. "And he's twice as ornery. The Mexicans killed his family a few years back, so he don't have too good an outlook on things. But near as I can tell he's an honorable man. Good as his word. But this Sanchez is another story. Hear tell he likes to kill just for the sake of killin'."

Levi's smile faded, and Hobbs turned for a last look at the fort. Already the adobe walls were no more than a shimmering image in the distance, then quickly lost from sight altogether as he and his men dipped into a shallow ravine dotted with prickly pear. Ahead, giant saguaros, arrayed like a random army of signposts, beckoned the soldiers with upturned arms to the open desert—and the Apaches.

A delivery wagon rumbled through the gray of a false dawn, and the *click-clack* of the swaybacked horse's hooves echoed off the grimy brick buildings that lined a deserted cobblestone Boston street.

The wagon stopped at a building surrounded by a high, rusting fence with a faded sign, BOSTON LATIN SCHOOL FOR BOYS. The driver wrestled a bag of coal to his shoulder, lugged it through the wrought-iron gate, and deposited it with a loud thud at the front door. Inside, J. Wentworth McAllister III, dressed in a knickers suit and shirt and tie, stood in a darkened, barrackslike room on the second floor watching the deliveryman from an open window. Then he went back to knotting a bedsheet around the frame of his bunk, first in a long row of bunks that ran the length of one wall. The rest were filled with sleeping boys whose gentle snores mingled with the sound of the coal bags dropping, then the retreating clatter of horseshoes on stone. One of the boys stirred, sat up, and rubbed his eyes.

"What are you doin', McAllister?" he whispered. "And how come you're all dressed in your good clothes?"

"Shh, Fatso. Please be quiet," Mac replied.

"My name ain't Fatso. It's . . ."

"I know, I know. I'm sorry, Harvey, it's just that . . ."

"So, what're you doin' with the bedsheets and all?"

"Shh. I'm going to see my father." Mac didn't like the tone of Fatso's voice; it sounded like trouble. He tugged at the stiff collar that was suddenly too tight. He hated this suit, right down to the high shoes that went with it. But if he was to have any chance to get in to see his father, he had to look his best.

"They don't let ten-year-old kids into the hospital," Fatso scoffed. He threw back his covers and exposed pudgy legs sticking out from under his nightshirt. The bed groaned as he swung his feet to the wooden floor.

"Father says you can buy yourself into anyplace," Mac whispered back, annoyed at Fatso's know-it-all tone but not wanting to get into an argument right now. This was no time for another fight.

Fatso had a cruel leer on his face. "I'm gonna tell."

"Please, Fatso," Mac pleaded, "I mean, Harvey. He's very sick, and I've just got to see him. I'll give you a dollar to keep quiet." Without waiting for an answer, he threw the knotted sheets out the window, where they hung like a long white tongue that nearly reached the ground.

"Five dollars," Fatso demanded.

Mac moved his bunk closer to the window and tugged at the first sheet, testing the knot at the bed frame. Then he glanced at Fatso. "That's a lot of money."

"You're always sayin' how rich your old man is." Fatso was on his feet now. He padded to Mac's side and looked out the window.

"Well . . ." Mac said, digging into a pocket of his knickers. "All right. But you've got to promise you won't tell where I went." He took out a leather wallet and, turning his back to Fatso, thumbed through a sheaf of bills and took out a five.

"What're ya hidin'?" Fatso wanted to know. "Maybe I ought to make it ten."

"You said five." Mac handed Fatso the bill. "A deal is a deal."

Smiling, Fatso took the money and started back to his bunk while Mac put his wallet away and climbed up onto the windowsill. He tested the sheets one more time, then began to lower himself down the side of the building. After just a few feet the knees and elbows of his suit were blackened from the soot and grime that clung to the ancient bricks. *Drat,* he thought as he worked his way down hand over hand, *if I get too dirty, they'll never let me into the hospital.*

When he was a couple of feet from the ground, he let go and dropped to the dirt below. In the first light of dawn he brushed at his elbows and knees, only to find that his hands were now as black as his clothes. He wondered if he could find someplace to wash. "The heck with it," he whispered after a moment's thought. "If I can sneak out of this old school, I can sneak into a dumb hospital."

Mac took a last look up at the dangling sheets. He was surprised to see Fatso framed in the open window, a wide, leering grin on his face. *What's he laughing at?* Mac wondered, and he started toward the cobblestone walkway leading away from the school. He didn't have to wonder long. As he rounded the corner of the building, he found himself staring into the slender, hawk-nosed face of Sister Vera, scowling down at him from under the cowl of her jet-black habit.

Dust devils, swirling like small tornados, whipped through the teddy bear cholla and blue sage and added another layer of fine powder to Hobbs' once-blue uniform. He and his men covered their faces with bandannas until the winds passed, then beat at their clothing with their hats. They were descending from a high mesa, heading for the valley floor that stretched for miles like a giant, blistering frying pan, a flatness broken only by an occasional stand of creosote bushes or prickly pear.

"This is a waste of time," Levi groused. "We ain't never gonna find no Apaches."

"We already did." Hobbs pointed to a distant rise across

the valley. A row of mounted horsemen, hardly more than dark shadows in the shimmering distance, sat motionless. Levi whistled silently. "Lordy! You can hardly see 'em. How long they been out there?"

"Half hour or so." Hobbs chuckled at the wide-eyed look on his corporal's face.

"Think they seen us?" Levi wanted to know

"Maybe, maybe not." Hobbs pointed again, this time at a forty-five-degree angle from where the Apaches sat watching. "They got other things on their mind." A wagon train, trailing a thin wisp of dust, was making its way across the valley floor. The wagons moved slowly as teams of horses, mules, and oxen labored in the midday heat.

Suddenly a chorus of piercing screams and shrieks carried on the dry desert air. Levi turned toward the sound. His eyes bulged, and his jaw dropped. "Look, Sarge!"

"I got eyes," Hobbs barked. The Apaches were moving in a fluid mass from their position on the ridge, riding at a full gallop toward the helpless wagon train on the valley floor. Hobbs raised his arm. "Forward at the gallop . . ."

"But, Sarge," Levi protested, "Cap'n Horner said . . ."

"Think I'm just gonna sit here and watch?" Hobbs shot back. "Besides, you're the one who wanted a fight. Maybe now's your chance." He put spurs to his horse's flanks. "Forward at the gallop, ho!" he commanded, and with dust swirling he led his men off the ridge in a headlong dash along a course intended to intercept the attacking Apaches.

Chapter Two

This was your second fight this week, Mac—and it's only Tuesday." Sister Elaina sat behind a small wooden desk, her wrinkled hands folded in front of her and resting on a stack of papers. From under the cowl of her habit, pale green eyes looked out from a still-pretty face lined now with age, and her voice was tinged with weariness.

An awkward stillness settled over the small, musty room. Mac rubbed at his ear. It ached from being pinched between Sister Vera's bony fingers as she had propelled him from the dormitory to the school administrator's office. Now she sat across from Sister Elaina's desk, glaring at Mac with her small, beady eyes.

"What are we going to do with you, Mac?" Sister Elaina asked quietly.

"I know what I'd do with him," Sister Vera said. "I'd . . ."

Sister Elaina stopped her with a sharp glance, then refocused her attention on Mac. He was pouting now and felt like he was being picked on. After a long silence he blurted, "It was a matter of honor. Fatso Flemington said . . ."

"I've asked you not to call him Fatso," Sister Elaina insisted, scolding Mac with the tone of her voice.

"Then make him stop saying bad things about my father. Besides, I paid him a lot of money not to tell."

"I realize," said Sister Elaina, "you're very concerned

10

about your father's health, but we just can't put up with these disruptions anymore. The fights, your repeated attempts to sneak out, your constant refusal to follow the rules, your—"

"Father says rules are for sheep," Mac interrupted.

Sister Vera took a big breath that sounded as if it would suck all the air out of the stuffy room, then opened her mouth to speak. But Sister Elaina stopped her with a sidelong glance and said to Mac, "Your father doesn't have to worry about running this school. Besides, he's counting on us to teach you right from wrong."

"Only God works miracles," Sister Vera said, just loud enough to be heard, and rolled her eyes toward the ceiling. She drew another sharp look from the administrator, who then said, "I'm afraid we're near the end of our rope with you, Mac."

Sister Vera appealed to the ceiling once more and crossed herself before breathing a whispered, "Amen."

Sister Elaina scowled at the other woman and motioned toward the doorway. "Thank you, Sister, you may leave us now."

Mac stifled a giggle as the red-faced nun, looking petulant, got to her feet and swept out the door. But his moment of glee was brief. The awkward silence that again settled over the room grew as heavy as the gathering dusk. He felt Sister Elaina's eyes bore into his. Her usually kind face was drawn tight, her mouth a straight line.

"This is your last chance, Mac." The tone of her voice made him shiver. "One more incident and I have no choice but to send you to live with your uncle."

Mac's heart sank. "But I want to be with my father."

"He's just too ill."

Mac felt a cold fear creeping over him. He struggled for something to say. Anything. Anything to make her change her mind. "You . . . you've got to keep me here!" he insisted. "My father paid you a lot of money to let me stay here. You can't . . ."

"True, your father made a very generous gift to this school." Sister Elaina's voice was quieter now, but Mac could still feel its steely firmness. "But there were no guarantees."

He got up and stood by her desk. "Please, I want to stay here. I hate Arizona."

"You've never been there."

"I don't care," Mac shot back, his bravado of a few minutes earlier beginning to crumble. "I . . . I hate it anyway." He fought back the tears welling in his eyes, determined not to let her see him cry.

"Your uncle is the only other family you have," Sister Elaina said.

"I hate him too," Mac insisted. "My father hates him."

Sister Elaina scowled. "We don't *hate* anyone."

Mac took a deep breath, desperate to make one last appeal to help insure against being kicked out of school. "I don't care. I want to stay in Boston," he demanded. Then he decided to try a different approach, to play for the nun's sympathy. "It's where . . ." He paused, trying to squeeze out a tear. "It's where my father is. I want to be here, near my father." He put on the saddest face he could muster. "Please?"

Sister Elaina's shoulders drooped, and she heaved a deep sigh. "You may stay here as long as you obey the rules. And no more fighting with Fatso—er, ah, Harvey." Her kindly face reddened. Mac stifled another giggle, and he and the nun stared at each other for a moment. Then he shrugged, unable to think of anything more to say.

When Sister Elaina finally spoke, her voice sounded ominous, made all the more threatening by the near darkness of the room. "But remember, Mac, this is your last warning."

He knew she meant it this time.

Chapter Three

Phil McAllister snapped the reins over the back of his team, urging them to a quicker pace as he turned the lumbering freight wagon down Benson's dusty main street. He rumbled past the stage depot and turned again at the saloon before heading for the feed store next to the blacksmith shop. Reining up, he let the horses drink briefly at the watering trough, then tied them at the hitching rail and made his way into the store. In a few minutes he emerged with a sack of grain over each shoulder and let them fall with a plop into the wagon bed. After several trips the wagon was loaded, and he was about to close the tailgate when a voice called out.

"Phil! Phil McAllister!"

He dropped the tailgate and turned to see Charlie Grubb, a tall, skinny man wearing sleeve garters and a green eyeshade, standing in the doorway of the telegraph office. Charlie waved as he half walked, half trotted across the street between a passing buckboard and a few men on horseback. "Phil," he yelled again, "there's a telegram for ya."

Phil wiped at his forehead with a bandanna while he waited. "It come for ya yesterday," Charlie said when he got to the wagon. He paused and tapped a thin finger on the folded paper he was holding. "From back East. 'Fraid it's bad news." At the words "bad news" a couple of passersby

14

stopped to stare, but Phil gave them a dark look, and they moved on.

"Your brother," Charlie said, lowering his voice. "He—he passed away. I'm sorry."

"Don't be," Phil snapped. Charlie's eyes widened, but Phil ignored his surprised look and wiped at the inside of his hat with the bandanna.

"That ain't all," Charlie added quickly. "Looks like your nephew's comin' to live with ya. Be here in 'bout a week or less."

"Now, that's what I call bad news," Phil grumbled, and he slammed the tailgate shut. He didn't like kids. Especially other people's kids. And in particular he didn't like his brother's kid, even though he had never met him. *Probably just like his old man,* he thought, *a pompous, rich snob.* At least he had been. *Don't guess he could take it with him. But you can't be sure with him.*

Charlie stood with his mouth open, and Phil wondered if he was waiting to catch flies in it. He finally had to hold out his hand for the telegram. "Mind if I read it for myself?" he said.

Charlie's mouth snapped shut, and he looked like he had just awakened from a quick nap. "What? Oh, yeah," he said, and he handed Phil the slip of paper. "I just thought you'd want to know as soon as . . . You know, fast as I could tell ya." He shrugged.

Phil stared at the scribbled message. "Guess it's true," he muttered softly, still not wanting to believe it, then stuffed the paper into a shirt pocket. He climbed up into the wagon, took up the reins, and urged the team into motion as he gave Charlie a last look and mumbled a halfhearted thanks.

Charlie's face sagged for a moment, and he seemed disappointed that the conversation was over. Then he brightened. "Hope he don't have no trouble with the Apaches on the way."

Phil reined up, felt his eyebrows rise.

"I hear a bunch of 'em are off the reservation," Charlie went on, obviously glad to be the bearer of more news. Then with a worried look he added, "I wouldn't leave the missus alone too long if I was you."

Though the day was blistering hot, Phil felt a chill and shivered. He clucked at his horses, snapped the reins sharply over their backs, and the wagon creaked slowly forward.

"Fire at will!" Hobbs yelled as he and his squad raced across the valley floor with weapons drawn. But the Apaches had already aborted their attack and begun to wheel their column away from the wagon train and the charging soldiers. Both Indians and troopers snapped off a few ineffectual shots as they broke off an engagement that never really got started. "Cease firin'!" Hobbs ordered as the Apaches retreated in the direction they had come from.

One of the Indians reined up. He was young but tall and muscular, naked to the waist, and wearing a breechcloth and knee-high moccasins. His sweating chest glinted like copper, and the flowing black hair under his headband hung to his shoulders. He shook an army-issue repeating rifle in the air and let loose a scream that Hobbs knew was intended to strike fear into the hearts of those who heard it.

"Hold your fire," Hobbs ordered as the troopers reined up; and the Apache, his face filled with arrogance and his eyes blazing hatred, advanced his pony a few steps in their direction. Hobbs prodded his own mount forward until he and the Indian were no more than a few paces apart, and he stared back into the piercing black eyes.

The brave held his rifle in one hand and pointed it menacingly at Hobbs. "We will meet again, black soldier," he said in Chiricahua dialect. "Next time I will kill you." Then he wheeled his horse and with another shriek galloped after his departing band.

"What'd he say?" Levi wanted to know after Hobbs reformed the men and was leading them at an easy lope toward the wagons in the near distance.

"Just somethin' about he's gonna kill me the next time he sees me," Hobbs said. He ignored Levi's startled look and picked up the pace toward the wagons.

Even with the rattle of equipment and the clop of the men's horses, he could make out the creaks and groans coming from the Conestoga wagons as his squad closed on the train. No wonder they called them prairie schooners, he thought. They not only looked like some kind of round-sailed ships to Hobbs, they even sounded like it. He found himself remembering the rasping and creaking of the lines that held the ships in Charleston Harbor on the night long ago after he had run away from the plantation and tried to hide aboard an outbound vessel.

A yell from the wagon train cut short his reminiscence.

"Hellooo!" called the young, plain-looking man who waved from the driver's seat of the lead wagon. He took off his broad-brimmed hat and used it to signal a halt to the wagons that followed, and cries of "Whoa!" rang out all along the train as it strained to a stop. The pretty woman beside him looked worried and kept her hands folded over her belly, large with child, as though to keep her precious cargo secure against the jolting and pitching of the wagon, not to mention the Apaches.

Hobbs halted the squad and advanced on the lead wagon alone.

"Howdy," the young man said. "I'm Aaron Wry, and am I glad to see you."

"I'm Sergeant Hobbs, Ninth Cavalry. Attached to Fort Huachuca." He eyed Aaron for a moment, taking note of the neat, Eastern-style clothes; certainly not the dress of the usual wagon train boss.

"This here's my wife, Cindy," Aaron said, and he motioned to the fair-haired woman next to him. She gave Hobbs a grateful look but said nothing as a pretty girl, about ten, her dark hair in pigtails, appeared from the depths of the wagon and squeezed into the seat beside her. "And this is Peg," Aaron added.

Hobbs touched his hat and nodded. "You in charge?" he said to Aaron, wondering if the real wagon master might have been out scouting the Apaches.

"Sort of," Aaron replied, his whiskered face twisting in a lopsided, friendly grin that Hobbs thought might be hiding a hint of embarrassment. "Just till we get to the fort. I'm the new sutler storekeeper."

"I didn't take ya for a regular wagon master," Hobbs admitted.

Aaron's face reddened slightly under his beard. "I can understand why. I ain't had much experience with Indians—especially ones tryin' to kill us."

"Ah, they're probably just hungry," Hobbs reassured him. "Or lookin' to steal some horses. They're not likely to bother ya now, long as they know there's soldiers around. But," he cautioned, "ya better keep rollin', just to be on the safe side."

Cindy slipped an arm around Peg's shoulders and squeezed closer to her husband. "Can you ride with us a ways?" Aaron asked.

"We got orders to keep movin'," Hobbs answered. "Our job's to follow them Indians to their camp." Then, seeing the worry on their faces, he said, "But we'll try to check on ya from time to time—whenever we can."

Aaron nodded and waved his hat again to the wagons behind him. "Let's get goin'!" he yelled. "Everybody stay closed up." He snapped a whip over the backs of his horses and urged them into a straining, creaking start while Hobbs signaled for his troopers to move out. Then, with a salute to the Wrys, he turned his horse away from the wagon train at a slow walk and cast a quick look across the valley toward the distant ridge.

The Apaches were nowhere to be seen.

A buckboard, pulled by an old, tired horse, left the traffic in the cobblestone street and angled toward the entrance to a busy railroad station. Sister Vera was at the reins; Mac pouted in the seat beside her. Seemingly without urging, the horse stopped at the curb and heaved a wheezing sigh.

The crowd at the station sent bits of conversation ebbing and flowing across the wooden platform beneath the brightly painted gingerbread façade that swirled around the sign reading BOSTON, MASS. Men in bowler hats and fine suits and carrying carpet valises strode among the bonnets and fancy, bustled dresses worn by ladies who shaded their delicate cheeks from the warm New England sun with colorful parasols. A gleaming coal-black engine chuffed patiently while porters, their dark faces shiny with sweat, loaded an assortment of bags and boxes onto coach platforms and into open doors.

Sister Vera scooped up her flowing habit with one hand and stepped nimbly to the ground. Mac watched glumly as she made her way to the back of the small wagon and began to wrestle with two large leather suitcases. Then he got down from the buckboard and, hands in his pockets, started toward the station platform. He looked back just in time to see Sister Vera, eyes snapping, set the heavy bags down and start in his direction. With a half dozen long strides she was at his side, the lobe of his left ear firmly in her grasp.

"Not so fast, young man."

Mac winced as she tugged him back to the buckboard. She gave his ear an extra twist and forced him to pick up one of the bags. "Why can't we get a porter?" he complained.

"Because I don't have money for a porter," the nun replied, and she grunted as she picked up the other bag.

"Well, I do."

"Humph!" Sister Vera snorted. "I'm sure you do. Better save it. You've got a long trip ahead of you."

This is stupid, Mac told himself, struggling with both hands to drag the bulky satchel. Father would never have been seen carrying his own bags. At the thought of his father, he felt again the now-familiar ache in his throat, and tears brimmed in his eyes. He slowed and set the bag down, but another pinch of Sister Vera's fingers stung him into motion again.

At the train, a jolly-looking porter, his plump face stretched in a wide white grin, tipped his hat to Sister Vera. "Howdy, ma'am. Name's Jim. Lemme give y'all a hand." He took the nun's bag and swung it easily up onto the platform of the nearest car. *That's more like it,* Mac thought, as Jim took his suitcase and tossed it up beside the other one. Then he gazed unhappily around the bustling platform, watching as people said hurried good-byes, and the panting of the engine grew louder. He paid little attention as Sister Vera dug out an envelope from somewhere in the folds of her habit and handed it to the porter.

"He's paid all the way."

"He sho' is," Jim agreed after he examined the ticket and handed the envelope back. "And don't you worry none, we'll see he gits there safe and sound. We ain't lost no passengers in—oh, two, maybe three weeks now." A chuckle shook Jim's huge belly, and his face was aglow again with a bright smile.

Mac scowled at him. *Very funny,* he thought. He was about to say as much when a whistle blast startled him, and he jumped. The sound was followed by a cry of "All aboard!" from somewhere toward the front of the train. "You best git on board, sonny," Jim said, his voice matching his gentle look.

Mac felt the hair rise on the back of his neck. "My name's not sonny. I'm J. Wentworth McAllister the third, and I don't need any colored help telling me what to do."

Sister Vera gasped. Jim's smile faded, and little hurt lines appeared at the corners of his big round eyes. Mac felt a need to lash out, a need he didn't quite understand. "My father owns this railroad," he blurted, "or did, before he . . . before he . . ." Mac swallowed hard, took a breath, then said, "I'll get on board when I'm good and ready."

Jim shrugged, and his smile reappeared, but it had lost

some of its warmth. "Well," he said quietly, "if you ain't good 'n' ready in 'bout two minutes, you gonna be left standin' here on the platform while the rest of us goes to Denver." Then he tipped his cap to Sister Vera, swung up onto the nearest car, and disappeared through an open door.

Mac waited for the reprimand he knew was sure to come. But when he turned to Sister Vera, he was surprised to see the usually harsh lines of her face softened into a sad, almost kindly mask.

"Don't make things so hard for yourself, Mac. Most people want to help you. Maybe even . . . maybe even be your friend. If you'll let them."

Looking suddenly embarrassed, she reached into her habit again and took out the envelope she had shown to Jim. She stuffed it into the breast pocket of Mac's jacket and patted it gently as though to make it secure. He was certain he felt her fingers linger in a momentary caress.

"Just show that to the man at the stagecoach office in Denver," she said, her voice suddenly husky. "It's your ticket to Arizona. Your uncle will meet you in Benson."

Mac stared into her face and tried to swallow but couldn't. Sister Vera reached out and, as she had often done over the past two years, took him by both shoulders. But this time there was a gentleness in her grip that he had never felt before, and he saw tears in her eyes.

"Good-bye, Mac. I'm sorry things . . . If only you had just . . ." She sighed. "Will you write?" she said, then added quickly, "To Sister Elaina, I mean."

Mac's lower lip began to tremble, and he couldn't control it. *Why should I?* he thought. *Why should I write to anyone? No one cares about me.* He turned quickly from Sister Vera's grasp and mounted the train steps, his eyes nearly blinded now by hot tears. He stumbled into the car, threw himself into the first of several empty seats, and leaned back against the coarse fabric of the headrest. As the train lurched into motion, he wiped at his cheeks and peered around, hoping no one had seen him cry. He was glad that the few passengers waving at friends or relatives on the platform were too busy to notice.

Mac sat up and looked out the window, the imperfections in the glass making wavy lines in the scene that was starting to slip slowly by. The train gathered speed, and he saw Sister Vera walking to keep pace, her upturned face pale against the cowl of her habit. As Mac's gaze locked with hers, she waved hesitantly, tentatively, as if not sure she really should. Then, unable to keep up, she stopped and made a hasty sign of the cross before she clutched her folded hands to her breast.

As the train pulled away, Mac strained forward to see her, his face pressed to the window. But now she was out of sight, and when he sat back, there were wet smudges on the glass, and he felt more alone than he ever had in his life.

Chapter Four

The sound of the whistle filled the rolling plains as the train wound its way through the gently rising foothills of the Great Divide. Thick black smoke billowed from the angular, funnel-shaped stack, and the engine strained to pull the cars ever upward toward the tree-lined mountains to the west.

In the dining car, Mac finished his last forkful of dark brown chocolate cake and looked around for the waiter. He felt a little sick to his stomach but was determined to have another helping, along with some smooth, thick whipped cream to go with it. After all, if he was being forced to leave Boston, he could at least have what he wanted to eat. He wiped his mouth on the linen napkin at his neck and took a swallow of water from the goblet next to his fine china plate. The delicate pattern in the glass matched the one etched into the small vase in the center of the table that held a cluster of rosebuds huddled in red contrast to the tablecloth, white and spotless except for the crumbs scattered around Mac's plate.

This is how my father would dine, he told himself, and he tried to think of some suitable rebuke for when the absent waiter reappeared. Just then a tall, slender black man, wearing a white jacket and carrying a large metal tray, entered the car. He began clearing dirty dishes from an empty table.

"Waiter!" Mac shouted, and he held up his hand and

snapped his fingers impatiently several times. This drew dark looks from the other diners seated nearby, but Mac ignored them. "Waiter!" he called again.

The black man looked up and started in Mac's direction, moving smoothly and with a practiced grace that offset the swaying motion of the car. "Yes, sir," he said softly when he reached the table, but Mac could see the resentment in his snapping eyes.

"More cake," Mac demanded.

"You sure your eyes ain't bigger'n your belly, young man?"

"That's none of your affair," Mac shot back, annoyed and embarrassed at being questioned in front of so many on-lookers.

"Yes, sir, but that's a lotta cake for one small boy," the waiter persisted, his voice growing sterner.

"I'm sick of people like you telling me what to do," Mac snarled. *I've had enough of this,* he fumed to himself, and he tore the napkin from his neck and threw it onto the table. *First that rude porter at the station and now this. I wish my father were here; he'd set them straight.* He brushed past the waiter and stalked to the door at the far end of the dining car.

"Sorry, sir," the waiter called, "that area's just for . . ."

But the man's words were lost in the hiss of compressed air that escaped from the automatic closing mechanism as Mac pulled open the heavy door. That sound was immediately replaced by the noise of rushing wind and the *click-clack* of the wheels, and he found himself on the train's rear observation platform, a small area surrounded by a railing of wrought-iron curlicues. At one side a low table was set with a white cloth, a plate of sandwiches and fruit, and an open bottle of whiskey and two partially filled glasses. Mac stood for a moment, swaying with the roll of the train, while he watched two men with rifles firing randomly at a small herd of buffalo that raced alongside, not more than fifty yards from the train tracks.

The men were expensively dressed, both wearing the latest in hunting jackets over their ruffled shirts, and their tailored twill breeches were tucked into shiny, knee-high riding boots.

"Great shot, Clyde," whooped the shorter, younger man, and he hoisted one of the glasses in mock salute and laughed. "I think you hit a prairie dog," he said, and he took a long drink.

"Can't get a steady shot," grumbled Clyde, looking somber. "It's the train."

"Or the sour mash," his partner said, following his words with more hoots of laughter.

"I haven't seen you hit anything," Clyde growled.

The young man's smile vanished. "Watch," he said, and he raised the repeating rifle to his shoulder, took long, careful aim, and fired. A spurt of dust erupted about ten feet in front of the lead buffalo, and the herd charged on unscathed.

"You led him too far," Mac said, feeling superior and confident in his assessment.

The men turned. The younger one smiled, but Clyde scowled and gave Mac a withering look. "Listen to that, will ya?" he growled. "Who are you, Buffalo Bill? Beat it, kid, this area's for grown-ups."

A kid, am I? Mac thought, and he squared his shoulders. "It so happens that I'm J. Wentworth McAllister the third, and my father . . ."

"McAllister?" Clyde said gruffly. "You any relation to old Wentworth McAllister from Boston?"

Mac nodded, feeling a flush of pride. "He was my father."

"That explains your smart mouth," Clyde shot back.

Mac was about to respond when the younger man said, "I didn't know old Mac had any kids." Then with a chuckle he added, "Or even a wife, for that matter."

Before Mac could decide whether or not he was being made fun of, Clyde barked, "Don't matter. Can't you see we're shooting here, sonny? Run along."

Mac was going to argue that his name wasn't sonny but changed his mind. Instead he said, "That rifle you're using is too light for buffalo."

To the obvious enjoyment of his partner, Clyde began to sputter. "Wha-What? Listen to that, will ya? I guess I ought to know what kind of rifle to use for what game."

"My father always told me . . ."

"Your old man never hunted in his life," Clyde scoffed.

"Well," Mac went on, determined to be heard, "he hired a shooting teacher for me, and . . ."

"I suppose that makes you an expert." Clyde held up his rifle. "For your information, this is a—"

"A Winchester '73," Mac broke in. "Lever action. Holds twelve rounds. With an extended barrel for greater accuracy."

Clyde's face was suddenly a red balloon as his cheeks puffed out and his eyes bulged. His companion doubled over with laughter.

"But," Mac continued, "it would still take a perfect shot to bring down a buffalo with it."

Clyde's face returned to its normal color, and his eyes narrowed. "Okay," he said, "you're so good, let's see you drop one."

He tossed Mac the gleaming weapon. He caught it easily, grateful now for the hours of practice he had put in at the side of the most respected firearms instructor in Boston. But the memory also brought a twinge of melancholy as he thought of the many times his father, despite solemn promises, had failed to show up at his training sessions. He forced the memories out of his mind and focused his attention on the rifle. It felt good in his hands, and he swung it to his shoulder and sighted along the smooth barrel, bringing it to bear on the leader of the herd that still thundered alongside the train.

Then he lowered it. "My father always told me you should only shoot an animal for food—or a man in self-defense." He raised the rifle again and pointed it at Clyde's chest. Clyde recoiled, like a puppet jerked on an invisible string, and slammed into the table, slopping whiskey out of the glasses. Mac lowered the rifle and offered it back.

"Just like your old man," Clyde said, recovering quickly, "all talk." He ignored the weapon in Mac's outstretched hands.

"I just don't believe in killing animals unless there's a good reason," Mac argued.

The younger man, still smiling broadly, grabbed the bottle from the table and went to the rear of the platform. "Here, kid, try this." He cocked his arm, ready to throw.

"Hey, that's my good bourbon!" Clyde said, and he lunged toward his companion. But he was too late. The bottle sailed in a high arc off the end of the train. Mac snapped the rifle to his shoulder, sighted, squeezed the trigger, and felt a rush of pride as the bottle exploded in midair. Casually, he levered the spent casing out of the chamber and handed the rifle back to Clyde, who, wide-eyed and speechless, took it without comment.

Mac stifled an urge to laugh and, with his shoulders squared and a swagger in his walk, headed back toward the dining car. He pried open the heavy door, paused, and turned to face the men. "It pulls a hair to the left," he said; then he stepped through the door and let it hiss closed behind him.

Geronimo sat astride his horse on the crest of a small hill and watched as a dozen or so Apache braves poured rifle fire onto a single-story adobe ranch house, their Winchester carbines and stolen army-issue Sharps repeaters belching smoke in the long rays of the afternoon sun.

By ones and twos the attackers moved forward: some to the edge of the large corral, some to the low stone wall twenty feet or so from the front door, others to the protection of a watering trough, but always advancing toward the house.

Geronimo squinted into the sun, searching for Sanchez. He spotted him next to the wall, eyes fierce in his coppery face and a sheen of sweat covering his naked chest. *Fool,* Geronimo said to himself, as Sanchez motioned the other braves to new vantage points. From behind the burlap hanging in the two dark windows, rifle muzzles appeared, fired quickly, and disappeared again. The Apache nearest Sanchez fell to the ground, twitched a few times, then lay still.

"Young fool," Geronimo grumbled aloud. "He won't be satisfied until we're all dead. And for what? A few horses."

While the Chiracahua chieftain watched, Sanchez stood erect, raised his rifle over his head, and screamed for his men to attack. They arose without hesitation and advanced on the building, crouching and firing their weapons from the hip. Sanchez was the first to reach the house, and the other Apaches stopped shooting. The sudden quiet hung like the dust and gun smoke that floated lazily in the late-afternoon heat. Then, with a shriek, Sanchez kicked down the wooden door and stepped through the opening into the darkness beyond. The silence was immediately torn by another scream, one that was high-pitched and filled with terror and cut short by two quick shots, then followed by more quiet.

Geronimo knew what had happened. He kicked his pony in the ribs and galloped toward the ranch. Seconds later he reined to a stop in front of the house and in one smooth motion slid to the ground. The Apaches who had gathered near the open doorway parted before him and stood in silent reverence as he strode through the splintered doorway.

A lifeless man lay facedown on the rough-sawn wood floor with Sanchez bending over him searching his pockets. A blond woman, pale in death, lay on her back a few feet away, a dark stain spreading over the bosom of her plain calico dress.

"Why did you do this?" Geronimo hissed. "You said you only wanted to steal the horses."

Before he answered, Sanchez took a few coins and a small knife from the dead man's pockets, looked at them, then threw them to the floor. His dark eyes burned in his round, smooth face as he got to his feet and glared at his chief. "They caught us. What were we supposed to do, run like old women? This is our land."

"This will only bring more soldiers."

"Ha," Sanchez said scornfully, "let them come."

Geronimo shook his head at the younger man's stupidity and, without speaking, turned his back on him and walked out of the room. Outside, he signaled for the waiting men to get mounted, then went to his own horse and swung into the stolen army saddle just as Sanchez came out of the house.

"You are young and foolish, Sanchez." Geronimo knew that criticizing him in front of the others was a risky thing to do, but he wanted him to feel the sting of humiliation. Maybe it would teach him a lesson.

Sanchez glared, his face a defiant mask that slowly melted into the look of a spoiled child. Without looking at the other braves, he walked stiffly to his horse, paused, and pointed to the filled corral. "What about them?" he said to Geronimo.

"Another time."

"I say we take them now."

"They will only slow us down." Geronimo was growing impatient. "The soldiers we saw cannot be far behind us. They must have heard the shooting."

"Ah," Sanchez scoffed, and he spat on the ground. "They will never be able to keep up with us—or even find us."

"They are buffalo soldiers," Geronimo said sternly, his voice rising. "They track like the Apache and are brothers to the desert." He was through talking. He wheeled his horse and with nothing more than a nod led his men away from the ranch house at a gallop. He knew Sanchez would follow—at least for now. But he couldn't ignore the question that had been nagging him for months. The question of how long would it be before he was challenged for the leadership of his small, and dwindling, tribe.

Hobbs put field glasses to his eyes and adjusted them to bring the distant hills as close as possible. The wisps of white smoke he had been watching were all but invisible now against the deepening shadows.

"Geronimo?" Levi asked.

Hobbs handed him the glasses. "I don't think so."

Levi peered through the binoculars for a moment, then handed them back. "Sanchez?"

"Could be." Hobbs put the glasses back into their case. "Near as I can tell, it was a signal to meet someplace."

"Near as you can tell?" Levi chided, his smile bright in the advancing dusk. "I thought you could read smoke."

"Smoke ain't the only thing I can read," Hobbs shot back, a little annoyed at his corporal's teasing in front of the men. "That's more'n I can say for some people." He glanced at Levi and felt a stab of regret as he saw a hurt look replace the younger man's smile. *No need to be mean to him,* Hobbs thought. *Especially since he ain't gonna like what I got to say next.* "Put out a couple of guards," he ordered brusquely, "and have the men make a cold camp."

The mounted soldiers groaned, then slowly, stiffly, began to dismount. "C'mon, Sarge," Levi protested, "no fires? The men ain't had a hot meal in three days."

Hobbs swung to the ground and stared at his corporal for a moment. Then, making sure the men could hear, he said, "What'd ya rather have, cold food in yer gizzard or an Apache arrow?"

Levi's eyes grew wide, but he didn't speak.

"We'll pick up their trail first thing in the morning," Hobbs added matter-of-factly, and he began to unsaddle his horse.

Chapter Five

The train stood patiently at the station with its bell clanging in the clear mountain air. The sign on the plain clapboard station read, DENVER, COLORADO—EL. 5280 FT.

Mac paused on the top step, eyeing the crowd, their faces upturned, searching the train for friends or loved ones. Most of the people on the platform were dressed in coarse western-type clothes compared to the fancier styles of the arriving passengers. Seeing the warm greetings and hearing the friendly yells filled him with a strange loneliness, which, as he surveyed the unfamiliar surroundings, was replaced by a twinge of uneasiness.

"Out of the way, sonny," a gruff voice commanded.

Mac turned. A short, middle-aged man, his belly threatening to break the watch fob stretched tightly across his vest, was trying to get around the two suitcases at the top of the steps. Mac snatched at the bags, struggling to move them so the man could pass.

"Ought to know better than to block the way," the man grumbled, and he gave Mac a hateful look. "Children today have no regard for other people," he added as he waddled down the steps. He hailed a conductor on the station platform, took his elbow, and steered him away from the train. "I'm Pierpont Ambrose," Mac heard him say before his voice was lost in the noise of the crowd.

Mac grabbed one of the suitcases and bounced it down the steps to the platform. As he turned for the other one, he saw Jim, the black porter, swing it easily down beside its companion. Surprised by this simple kindness, Mac was at a loss for words.

"I . . . I'm . . . Thanks." He felt suddenly guilty for the way he had spoken to him at the station in Boston. Jim nodded, his smooth black face showing no emotion. As he turned to go, Mac blurted, "I . . . I'm sorry. I . . ."

Jim stopped and looked back. Then he pointed to a small frame building about twenty yards beyond the station. "Stage office is right over there. What there is of it." Then he climbed up the steps and disappeared into the train.

Mac left the bags and headed for the building. It was little more than a shed, with a hand-lettered sign that identified it as the Overland Stage ticket office. The sign was written on a wooden shutter that was propped open over a small window. A grizzled man who Mac suspected to be at least ninety leaned on his elbows in the opening, watching the people milling around the coach and six-horse team that stood nearby.

Mac handed him the envelope Sister Vera had given him. "My fare is paid all the way to Benson, Arizona."

The old man squinted at Mac, then took the ticket out of the envelope, thumped it with a big, official-looking stamp, and handed it back. "You travelin' alone, young fella?"

"Of course," Mac replied, standing as tall as he could. "See that my bags are taken care of, please." He pointed in the direction of his luggage. "They're over there by the train."

"Then you'd better tramp right on back and get 'em." The man smiled a toothless smile and cackled. "They ain't nobody here to tote your stuff. And the stage leaves in fifteen minutes."

"But I can pay," Mac insisted, feeling a rising anger.

The old man began to lower the wooden shutter, slowly, deliberately. "Fifteen minutes," he repeated, and he let it slam closed.

"But I've got money!" Mac yelled. "I can pay!" He pounded on the shutter, but there was no answer. *Why doesn't anybody listen to me?* he fumed silently. He kicked at the shed, sending a sharp pain through his foot, and as the uneasy feeling returned, he started, shoulders sagging, back to the train.

By the time he managed to half-carry, half-drag his suitcases to the waiting stagecoach, sweat had wilted the stiff collar at his neck. Now the stares and sidelong glances of the men and women standing at the coach embarrassed him. He saw the fat man, Pierpont Ambrose, in the group, and his resentment rose again. *He wouldn't get away with yelling at me if Father were here,* Mac consoled himself. Just then a short, husky man, wearing a battered Stetson and a buckskin jacket, pushed his way through the knot of people. His wrinkled face was the color of a new saddle, and his eyes seemed to be in a perpetual squint, as though looking into a bright sun. The corners of his mouth were dark—from chewing tobacco, Mac suspected. The janitor at school used to spit gobs of black juice into the fire when he tended the furnace in winter. He let Mac and Fatso try "a chaw" one time—it tasted awful.

"Howdy, folks." The man's voice made Mac think of sandpaper. "My name's Gus Milner, and I'm yer driver." He jerked a thumb at the tall, spindly black man behind him.

"And this here's Mushy. He'll be ridin' shotgun once we git out a ways."

Mushy grinned, and his dark eyes flashed beneath the floppy brim of his hat. He tossed a double-barreled shotgun and an oilskin rain slicker up into the front seat of the coach and began to collect the baggage.

Three men, including Ambrose, and a plain but pleasant-looking woman moved to the door as Gus and Mushy began putting bags into the boot at the rear of the coach and up on the roof, where they secured them behind a low metal railing. Mac hung back, and as he watched the grown-ups wedge themselves into the narrow seats, the thought of riding in the small, cramped area was suddenly very unpleasant, almost frightening. He went to Gus, who was handing the last piece of luggage up to Mushy.

"I want to ride on top." Mac tried to make his voice sound as grown-up as possible.

Gus turned, and his eyes squinted so tightly, Mac wondered how he could see at all. But the look was frightening. "Against the rules," he growled, and he pulled out a gold watch that was attached to his shirt pocket by a chain and checked the time. He stared at Mac again for what seemed like a long while, then said, "Let's go, sonny."

Mac bristled. "My name's not sonny. And I don't want to ride in that stuffy old coach." He reached for his wallet, took out several dollar bills, and held them out to Gus. "I want to ride on top, please," he repeated. It was more of an order.

Gus' squint widened just enough to reveal what looked like hot coals where his eyes should have been. Mac's outstretched hand began to tremble. "Look, sonny," Gus rasped, "either you git on board now, or we go without ya. And I don't much care either way." Then he turned and climbed nimbly up into the driver's seat.

Mac's face grew hot, and he knew without looking that every eye on the coach was trained on him. He put the money and wallet away just as he felt himself being scooped up by a pair of strong hands. "It ain't so bad, kid," Mushy said with a grin. "Least you'll be by the window." He set Mac gently into the last remaining coach seat—right next to Ambrose. "Wait'll we hit the desert in a couple days," Mushy added. "You'll be glad ye're inside."

Mac wanted to argue, but before he could say anything, Mushy was gone. Then he heard the snap of the reins, a whistle, and Gus' gravelly voice.

"Hahhh! Git up, team!"

The coach jolted into motion. The Denver train station began to pass from view, slowly at first, then more rapidly. Now Boston—and his father—seemed farther away than ever. Mac hated the stagecoach; he hated Gus; he hated the thought of Arizona. He wanted to cry.

Aaron Wry shaded his eyes against the fiery ball that settled lower in the west as it turned the wispy clouds on the horizon into ribbons of brilliant pink and orange. He shifted in his seat, handed Cindy the reins, and, without speaking, swung down from the wagon. He walked alongside the team for a few minutes, glad to be free of the hard, bone-crunching seat and letting the exercise ease the stiffness in his back.

He looked up at his wife and smiled; she smiled back. He marveled at how she managed to spend hour after hour in the merciless heat, sometimes riding inside, sometimes walking, and sometimes, like now, driving the team, but never complaining. He knew she had to be very uncomfortable most of the time, what with her extra weight. And recently she had had some unusual pains from time to time. *I hope everything's all right with the baby,* he fretted, then put the thought out of his mind.

Aaron scanned the distant hills that were turning purple now in the fading light. He saw a thin wisp of smoke and felt an icy fear clutch at his chest. *I wonder if that's what I think it is.* He looked back at the wagons strung out behind him and took off his hat and waved it. "Circle the wagons," he yelled. "We'll stop here for the night."

With much creaking and groaning and cries of "Whoa," the wagons began to bunch up and form a big loose circle. Men, women, and children climbed down from their perches, all rubbing aching backs and sore behinds that had been partially numbed by hours of jouncing in the hard seats. Toddlers scampered in all directions and squealed with delight at a few moments of freedom while their elder brothers and sisters joined their parents to help unhitch the teams, break out food and supplies, erect tripods to hang cook pots on, and begin watering their stock. Aaron was glad to see that everyone worked quickly and quietly—everyone except Loren Pike.

"What're we stoppin' for, Wry?" Pike demanded as he left his wife struggling with his team's bulky harness and strode in Aaron's direction. Pike's narrow face was pinched in a frown, and his small green eyes snapped under the brim of his dusty hat. *He reminds me of a snake,* Aaron thought, as Pike's tongue darted out and licked nervously at his thin lips. "Last night it was the rain," Pike whined. "What's your excuse this time? There's another good hour of daylight left."

Aaron disliked Pike intensely. The man was a complainer and a troublemaker. And Aaron couldn't stand the way he treated his wife, Liz. Not that she was much better. A thin, faded beauty of a woman with straggly blond hair, she mostly gave as good as she got, but the other women in the wagon train couldn't understand why she put up with Pike's constant verbal mistreatment and degradation that often stopped just short of physical abuse. But that was her business, Aaron decided; he had all he could handle just trying to get the wagons safely across the desert.

"That's right," he told Pike, "we got an hour of daylight left, and we'll need just about all of it to get supper and secure the wagons for the night."

"What're ya talkin' about?" Pike snarled. "Secure the wagons from what?"

Aaron pointed to the smoke in the distance, standing out clearer now against the backdrop of purple shadows creeping up the mountains.

"Humph!" Pike snorted. "You worried about a little smoke?"

Aaron ignored him and helped Cindy down from the wagon, then swung Peg down behind her. Cindy gave Pike a dark look but didn't speak. She put a protective arm around Peg's shoulders and steered her toward the back of the wagon while Aaron began to unhitch the team. "I'm worried about who might be sendin' that smoke," he said to Pike without looking at him. "Remember what that army sergeant said." He turned in time to see Pike's look grow dark, his eyes showing a glint of fear.

Aaron looked around the circle of wagons. "Close up a little tighter," he yelled to the other drivers. "Then get your animals fed and watered as soon as possible." When he moved to the front of his team, Pike followed him and just stood watching as he undid a piece of harness. "You'd better see to your stock," Aaron said finally, hoping he wouldn't have to put up with one of Pike's arguments.

"Look, Wry, I got business in California that won't keep."

Aaron finished unharnessing the horses and led them out of the traces.

Pike gripped his arm. "You hear me, Wry? I got business . . ."

"I'm more concerned about the business we got right here," Aaron shot back, anger creeping into his voice. He stopped his horses and looked toward Pike's wagon, where Liz was struggling to get the harness off her animals' backs. "She could use a little help," he told Pike.

Pike's eyes turned to green slits. "That's my affair," he hissed. Then his lips peeled back into what Aaron guessed was supposed to be a grin, exposing a row of uneven, discolored teeth. "Besides," Pike said with a humorless chuckle, "I ain't about to start spoilin' her now."

Aaron felt the hair rise on the back of his neck. How could any man be that ornery? And to his wife? Aaron's anger rose to the point where he had an urge to hit Pike, and he felt his hands knotting into fists. Struggling for control, he let out a long breath and said quietly, "See to your stock."

After Aaron secured his team, he went to a barrel lashed to his wagon and began to draw water into a wooden bucket. Pike scowled but said nothing, then started toward his own wagon. After a few paces he stopped, then turned to look at Aaron. "You really think that's Indian smoke?"

"What I think is," Aaron answered, trying to hide his annoyance, "the sooner we all get settled for the night, the better off we'll be."

Now Pike looked worried. Aaron couldn't help but feel a flush of pleasure at the sight, but he took his bucket of water and headed to where Cindy was building a fire out of dried sage twigs while Peg set up a tripod and cook pot.

"What were you and Pike talking about for so long?" Cindy asked.

He looked at his wife for a long moment and thought about how much he loved her. Again he wondered how Pike could be so thoughtless and cruel to Liz. Cindy's face took on a questioning look while she waited for Aaron to answer.

"Oh," he said, feeling suddenly playful, "I was just tellin' him how happy you'd be to have him join us for supper."

Cindy's eyes turned to crystals of blue ice, and she scowled. "I'd throw it on the ground first."

In spite of her tone, Aaron laughed, amused at how he had been able to rile her so easily. "Don't I recall the Good Book sayin' somethin' about lovin' your neighbors?" he teased.

"Pike makes it hard to remember," Cindy replied, her eyes snapping.

Aaron chuckled, went to his wife, and gave her a quick kiss on the cheek. Cindy's frown gave way to a smile, and the ice in her eyes melted. "You did that on purpose," she said in mock anger. Aaron nodded, put an arm around her shoulders, and looked toward the mountains again. Cindy's face grew serious as her gaze followed his to the faint trails of smoke still hanging in the gloaming.

"I saw it earlier," she said, her voice a little more than a whisper. "Do you think it's . . . ?"

Aaron felt her shudder. "We'd better eat," he said calmly, and he handed her the water bucket. She stared back at him for a moment, then poured water into the kettle while Peg spread tin plates and spoons on a blanket near their wagon.

Chapter Six

Mac lost track of how many days they had been riding. He vaguely remembered traveling through majestic ever-greens and the craggy mountains of Colorado that had now given way to the flat, seemingly endless brown of the desert—and the heat. Mushy had been right. As hard and as cramped as the seats in the coach were, Mac was glad to be inside. He had never felt the sun so hot or seen it so bright; the glare of the sandy landscape burned his eyes. He had long since taken off his jacket and tie and opened his wilted collar, and he had pushed down his long socks and unbuckled his knickers at the knees. Yet he still felt he might not be able to take another breath of fiery air.

He looked into the faces of the other passengers. Everyone else was sleeping, or nodding, eyes closed, their heads flopping from side to side or hanging on their chests. Mr. Ambrose was snoring. His fat jowls sagged, and with each jolt of the coach he slid closer to Mac, jamming him tighter against the frame of the small window. He retaliated with a sharp elbow to Ambrose's ribs. The man snorted, straightened up, stuck his feet into Mac's space, and resumed snoring.

Now Mac felt like he would die from boredom—if the heat didn't get him first. *Look at them,* he thought. *What a bunch, all sleeping. Not even anyone to talk to. Not that I'd want to talk to them anyway. Especially old Ambrose. I wish he'd move his big feet.* Mac studied the man's high-top shoes, clearly expensive, the fancy leather reaching well above his ankles; then he got an idea.

Checking to make sure the others were still dozing, Mac leaned over and untied Ambrose's shoelaces and carefully undid them from the little hooks on the upper part of his shoes. Ambrose stirred but then began snoring again. Scarcely breathing, Mac tied a lace from the right shoe to one from the left, then sat back and smiled. Somehow the air seemed a little cooler now. Still smiling, he closed his eyes and tried to sleep.

He wasn't sure, but it seemed like no more than a few minutes had passed before he heard Gus yell, "Whoa!" and the coach clattered to a stop. They were in front of a small adobe house with a roof made of ocotillo poles and a wooden door that was cracked and bleached white by the sun. The windows were small, glassless, dark holes in the walls.

The other passengers struggled awake, yawning and stretching. Ambrose grunted and took a limp handkerchief from his pocket and dabbed at the moisture across his forehead and upper lip. "I don't know how much more of this I can take," he wheezed.

"Just one more day, Mr. Ambrose," said the woman across from him, and she smiled as she moved to the door.

"Might as well be another year," Ambrose replied, and he grunted as he pulled himself upright in his seat.

Mac squeezed out of the coach right after the woman, then stood watching while the other passengers stepped down and followed Gus and Mushy toward the adobe house. He heard Ambrose grunt again inside the coach; then his

huge bulk appeared in the doorway, filling the small opening. He tried to take a step, realized he couldn't, and, clawing
the air and yelling, thudded facedown into the dust.

Mac laughed out loud as Gus and Mushy turned and ran
to Ambrose. "You gotta watch that first step," Mushy said,
trying to hide a smile.

"It wasn't the step," Ambrose hissed as he dabbed at his
face and spit dirt out of his mouth.

"Kinda looks like ya mighta tripped over your shoelaces
comin' out the door," Gus suggested. Ambrose gave him a
withering look and began to untie his shoes. Mac giggled at
the sight and started after the other passengers. Paying no
attention to their dark looks, he pushed in front of them and
was first in the door of the adobe house.

Inside he was met by a plump, gray-haired woman of
about fifty whose jolly face was lit by a smile. "Well, howdy.
I'm Missus Burns. Glad to see ya lookin' so happy, it bein'
so hot and all."

Her comment reminded Mac of how hot and uncomfortable he was, and he suddenly felt hungry and grumpy. "What
makes you think I'm happy?"

"Well, you was just grinnin' like a jackass eatin' briars.
If you ain't happy, then somethin' musta struck your funny
bone."

"Nothing that concerns you," Mac said, and he took a seat
at a large table set with tin plates, knives, and forks, platters
of tortillas and beans, and two huge pies. "I'd like to eat
right away," he announced as the rest of the passengers
approached the table, followed by Gus, Mushy, and a dusty
Mr. Ambrose.

"Soon's the other folks set down," Mrs. Burns said, her
smile replaced by a quizzical look. Within moments the

dim room fell quiet except for the sounds of eating. In between stuffing bites of food into his mouth, Ambrose cast hateful glances at Mac but said nothing. Later Mrs. Burns poured coffee from a large earthen pot while everyone finished off their meal with pie.

"What kind is it?" Mac wanted to know, after he coaxed her into giving him an extra piece.

"Prickly pear."

It was sweet and cool, and Mac gulped it down in a half dozen bites. *Sister Vera would skin me alive,* he thought, *if she saw me eating this way,* and he was amused by the image of her consternation. He was about to complain that he was the only one not offered any coffee but changed his mind. There was something else he wanted.

"More pie, please." It was a demand more than a request.

"Now, dearie," Mrs. Burns said, "you already had two big . . ."

"I can count, thank you." Mac reached for his wallet. "If it's the money you're worried about . . ."

"Goodness, gracious," Mrs. Burns said, looking hurt, "it ain't that, child."

"She don't want ya bouncin' around in that coach gettin' sick." Mac turned to see Gus glaring at him from under his heavy eyebrows. "And neither do I."

Mac could feel every eye in the room glaring in his direction, and he was suddenly embarrassed. He stared at Gus for a moment but was no match for his cold gaze, and he looked away quickly. Stuffing his wallet into his pocket, he pushed back from the table and stomped out the door. He had forgotten about the heat. It hit him like a wall, as if it had form and weight, even though the fading afternoon was being turned to an early night by a bank of angry black clouds piling up on the western horizon. Now more than ever the thought of getting back into the cramped, crowded coach actually made Mac a little sick to his stomach. Or was it—maybe—the pie?

No matter; he climbed to the top of the coach and found a space to sit between the bags. A breeze fanned his face; hot as a dragon's breath but a breeze nevertheless. He closed his eyes, and his belly grumbled. *Maybe if I could ride up here,* he thought, *it might be cooler after dark. I might feel . . .*

"All right, sonny, down." It was Gus.

"It's too hot to ride inside," Mac protested.

Mushy appeared next to Gus and grinned up at Mac. "Hot? You ain't seen hot. Wait'll we hit the real desert tomorrow; you'll think this was the North Pole."

Gus mounted a wheel hub of the coach, reached up to Mac, and swung him down into Mushy's outstretched arms. "Hot. Cold. Don't matter. You ride inside like everyone else."

Mushy held the door for Mac to get in. And as Gus stepped down from the wheel hub, a streak of lightning skipped across the blue-black horizon and was followed in a few seconds by a deep rumble.

"Bad sign," Gus said, as Mushy closed the coach door, "thunderstorm this time o' year."

"Horse feathers," Mushy scoffed. "You're gettin' as superstitious as an old woman."

"Yeah, well, you just get that scattergun out and keep yer eyes open," Gus said as he started for the driver's seat. "This could be a long night."

Mac awoke to sharp pains in his belly. At first he didn't know where he was. Everything was black, and there was a strange drumming noise that made him think of the sound of pelting rain. As the lurching of the coach brought him out of his stupor, he realized it was night and that it was indeed raining—hard. Someone had rolled down the canvas curtains over the windows, but they did little to keep out the water, and every few seconds flashes of lightning turned the inside of the coach blue-white. Thunder cracked and rumbled, momentarily drowning out the sound of the pouring rain.

Mac looked around, amazed that he was the only one awake. He crossed his hands over his belly and rocked back and forth in rhythm with the swaying coach. He felt sick, real sick, and he needed fresh air. He pushed aside a curtain and stuck his head out the window and let the rain beat on his face. It was cool, though the drops stung his cheeks. *I've got to get out,* he thought, and he forced his shoulders through the small opening.

Lightning flashed again, and he caught a glimpse of Mushy slumped in the driver's seat, his neck drawn down into the collar of his slicker. Water sprayed off his drooping hat, and his head lolled back and forth. Mac was sure he was sleeping and that this would be a good time to try to get to the top of the coach. The rain and the cooler air might make him feel better.

He twisted his body out the window and reached up, clawing for the metal railing that ran around the baggage rack. He clutched at it with both hands, but the rolling and bouncing made it hard to get a firm grip on the slippery metal. With enormous effort he freed his legs from the window and, drenched with water, struggled frantically to get a toehold on the side of the coach. Just as one foot found a secure position, a stabbing pain in his belly doubled him over, and one hand slipped from the railing at the same moment that he lost his footing.

The rattle of the coach and the clatter of the horses' hooves pounded in his ears, and panic threatened to choke off his breathing as he dangled by one hand from the lunging coach. His heart felt like it would burst from his chest in fear. He screamed for help, but the cry was lost in another crack of thunder. As lightning danced off the shiny wetness of the coach, Mac's hand slipped from the baggage rail, and he tumbled into the night. He was aware of the shock of hitting the ground for just an instant before he sank into a deep well of pain, then blackness.

Mac opened his eyes, then closed them again quickly; even through his eyelids the bright sun hurt. He explored his parched, rough lips with the tip of his tongue and gingerly felt the swelling on the back of his head where he had landed when he fell from the coach. He wasn't sure how long he had wandered in the desert since then, but he remembered walking and walking; it seemed like forever. And now all he could think of was how hungry and thirsty he was. He had stopped to rest under some scraggly bushes that smelled like some kind of medicine, and he must have fallen asleep. But now the sun had moved, and he was no longer in the shade, and the heat was nearly unbearable.

Mac struggled to his feet and immediately felt dizzy, in danger of falling. He sat down again and, almost without realizing he was doing it, began to cry. He was lost and scared. *Why didn't I just stay in the coach?* he thought. *I wish my father were here. I wish . . . I wish I were back in Boston, even back in school.* He moved into the shade of the bush again and lay down and closed his eyes. A vision of Sister Vera swirled through his head, and she was smiling, holding her arms out to him. "Time to turn in, Mac," she said gently, and she motioned him to his old, familiar bunk. Mac eased under the covers, but they were too warm, and when he closed his eyes, Sister Vera tucked them around his neck. Now the covers were stifling. "I'm so hot," he told her, and he tried to push the heavy blankets away, but he was too tired, too weak, and he drifted into a deep, tormented sleep.

Chapter Seven

L ook!" Levi shouted. "By that clump of creosote. There's someone out there."

Hobbs raised a hand, reined up, and the troopers behind him followed suit. "You men wait here," he said, and he and Levi spurred their horses toward the small stand of greasewood.

"Good Lord, he's just a boy," Hobbs said as he skidded his horse to a stop and slid from the saddle.

Levi climbed down beside him. "Pretty fancy duds, Sarge. Whattaya think he's doin' out here all alone?"

Hobbs gave Levi a quick glance and wondered how he could act so smart sometimes and ask such dumb questions at other times. "He might just tell us that, Corporal," he said, putting a hand to Mac's forehead, "if it ain't too late." The boy's skin felt hot, dry. He moaned softly as Hobbs picked him up as gently as he could and held him in his arms. "Let's git him over to the horses; looks like he could use some water."

At the horses, Levi shaded Mac's face with his hat while Hobbs held a canteen to his lips. A little water ran into Mac's mouth, but most of it spilled down his chin. He moaned weakly but didn't open his eyes.

"He looks pretty bad, Sarge," Levi offered.

This time Hobbs allowed as to how his corporal was

right. "And he's gonna look a lot worse if we don't find someplace to git him outa this sun."

Levi scanned the horizon in all directions. "We ain't exactly blessed with a lotta shade."

I can't argue with that, Hobbs said to himself; then he got an idea. He carried Mac to his horse. "If the mountain won't come to Mohammed " he muttered, thinking out loud.

"What?" Levi said, a perplexed look on his face.

"I know where there's shade," Hobbs said, as he climbed into his saddle with Mac cradled in his arms. "Let's go." He kicked his horse into action and motioned for Levi and the rest of the squad to follow.

In less than an hour they were in sight of the wagon train. Through the shimmering haze, Hobbs saw Aaron Wry wave his hat in a signal for the train to halt. As the soldiers approached, Aaron and several worried-looking men and women, with a few children among them, left the wagons and came out to meet them. No one spoke, but Hobbs could tell by their faces that they were wondering whether the boy in his arms was dead or alive.

Hobbs reined up at the rear of Aaron's wagon, where Cindy and Peg stood waiting, their eyes betraying their concern. "What on earth?" Cindy said, clutching her hands to her bosom. "Is he . . . ?"

"He'll live," Hobbs assured her. "We found him a few miles back," he explained, while Aaron opened a canvas flap at the back of the wagon.

"Where do you want him?" Aaron said to Cindy.

"On those blankets, next to where Peg sleeps."

"Ma!" Peg protested.

"Hush. Just for now," her mother said.

Hobbs put Mac in the wagon, then climbed in behind him and made room for himself among some chests, tools, and small pieces of furniture. He felt Mac's forehead again and loosened some of his clothing. Cindy helped him arrange Mac on the blankets. "How bad is he?" she asked.

"'Less I miss my guess, he's dried out pretty good. Probably passed out from the heat. His shoes are all scuffed and tore, like he's hiked quite a ways."

Aaron handed Hobbs a water canteen, and he held it to Mac's lips, but again the water just dribbled down his chin. "Don't seem likely he's been out there too long," Hobbs added. "Nobody'd last more'n a couple days without water."

"How do ya think he got here?" Aaron asked.

"From the bumps and bruises," Hobbs said, "I'd guess he fell off a horse, or a wagon maybe."

"Way out here?" Cindy said. "And dressed like that?"

"You got a point," Hobbs conceded.

A groan from Mac interrupted the conversation. "Maybe he'll tell us here in a minute or two," Hobbs said as Mac's eyes fluttered open and he stared around blankly, licking the water off his lips. Hobbs held up the canteen again. This time Mac swallowed a few times before water trickled out of his mouth.

Suddenly he bolted upright, his eyes opened wide. One by one he stared intently into the faces looking back at him. "Who are you? Where's the stagecoach? Where's Gus? And Mushy?"

Aaron chuckled, glanced at Hobbs and Cindy, then turned back to Mac. "So that's how ya got here. Well, I can answer one of those questions. I'm Aaron Wry, and this," he said, pointing at Cindy, "is my wife." Then he nodded at Hobbs. "And this is Sergeant Hobbs. He's the one who found ya."

Hobbs held out the canteen, and Mac took it without offering any thanks or showing any sign of gratitude. *Not much for manners,* Hobbs thought. Mac took a long drink of water, then with a gagging sound spit it out over the back of the wagon.

"Ahhgh! That tastes awful!"

Hobbs bristled at this lack of gratitude and grabbed the canteen just as Mac was about to let it fall to the ground. "I know it don't taste like sarsaparilla, kid, but out here it's too precious to spit into the dirt."

Mac gave Hobbs a defiant look but said nothing as he climbed awkwardly over the tailgate and slid to the ground. He seemed about to fall and clutched at the rear of the wagon to steady himself. The small crowd of people who had gathered formed a semicircle around him and stood gaping as if watching a sideshow in a carnival. Hobbs climbed to the ground and stood beside Aaron and Peg while Cindy watched from the wagon.

Mac looked at Aaron. "I've got to get to Denver—get the train for Boston."

There were snorts of laughter from the crowd. Aaron patted Mac's head. "'Fraid your compass is broke, son. Denver's back that way." He jerked his thumb toward the rear of the train. "We're headin' west. Fort Huachuca. Some folks are even goin' to California."

Loren Pike elbowed his way out of the crowd, a scowl on his bony face. "And we're wastin' time, Wry. We got three good hours of daylight left, so let's git goin'."

"Takin' a few minutes to help this young fella ain't exactly what I'd call wastin' time," Aaron replied, an angry edge in his voice.

Pike ignored the murmur of agreement from the circle of

people. "We voted you to lead the wagons," he said, "not play nursemaid to every stray you find along the trail."

I'd sure like to be countin' on him for help if I was lost, Hobbs thought as he eyed Pike and listened to the exchange between him and Aaron.

Mac went to Pike and clutched at his shirt. "You've got to take me back," he said, his voice trembling. "I'll pay you." Pike's scowl disappeared, and he eyed Mac with sudden interest. "I will," Mac went on. "I've got money." He reached into a pants pocket, then another one, then into his shirt, then into his pants again. His eyes were filled with a fear bordering on panic.

Pike's scowl returned, darker than ever. "Yeah," he said, his voice scornful and mocking, "sure ya do."

Mac's eyes brimmed with tears, and his voice cracked. "I've got money, I tell you. My father was rich." Now Pike's cackle was cruel, tormenting, and Mac, tears streaming down his cheeks, began to beat on his skinny frame with his fists. "I insist you take me back, do you hear? I'm rich. I can pay you!"

Pike's thin lips twisted into a snarl, and he grabbed Mac by the shirtfront. "I'll pay ya, ya little brat," he said, and he pulled back his hand, ready to strike.

Hobbs was between them in two quick steps and pushed Mac to safety while he gripped Pike's wrist with all his strength. Pike winced in pain and glared at Hobbs, the hatred in his eyes plain to see.

Aaron moved to separate them. "Hold on there, Pike. He's just a child. And a lost one at that."

Pike glowered at Aaron and then Hobbs. Rubbing his wrist, he nodded toward Mac and said, "He can stay lost for all I care. My concern is gettin' to California. The sooner the better." Then he strode off in the direction of his wagon.

Mac tugged at Aaron's sleeve. "But you've got to take me back." His voice was weak, pleading. "Please, I can . . ." His eyes rolled up under their lids, and he wavered for a moment, like a reed in the wind, and began to crumple.

Aaron caught him before he hit the ground and carried him back to his wagon and laid him on the blankets. Cindy dampened a cloth with water from a canteen and began to moisten his face and lips.

"He's probably starved," she said, as Hobbs approached. He took Aaron's arm and led him to the side of the wagon.

"I gotta get goin'," he said.

Aaron nodded that he understood. "What about the boy?"

"Will ya take him to the fort?"

"Why, sure, but . . ."

"Maybe ya can look after him till Cap'n Horner finds out who he is or where his folks are." In spite of Mac's ungrateful ways, Hobbs felt a twinge of pity for him, especially after the way Pike had treated him. Maybe it was because of the memories of his childhood in the days after his own father died. How he would have welcomed even the tiniest show of kindness.

Aaron looked hesitant, doubtful. "I—I can't promise. My wife's been having a pretty hard time. I'm not sure she's up to takin' care of another young'n right now. Besides, them Apaches scared her pretty bad. If you hadn't been around to run 'em off, I don't know how she woulda made out."

"I'll tell ya what," Hobbs said. He put a hand on Aaron's shoulder. He liked this man; he felt he could trust him. "You take the boy, and we'll ride with ya until we're sure you're outa danger."

Aaron shrugged, his face still clouded with doubt, but at last he nodded. Hobbs left him and returned to where Levi and the squad stood waiting by their horses. "Let's go," he said, and Levi gave the order for the troopers to get mounted. Hobbs saluted Aaron and Cindy and told them, "We'll be close by; just keep movin." Then Aaron gave the customary signal, and the wagon train groaned into motion.

Hobbs ordered the squad to move out along with the train, about twenty yards off its right flank. Levi questioned him with a look. "We're gonna ride with them for a ways," Hobbs informed him.

"I thought we was supposed to be lookin' for Geronimo."

"He'll keep," Hobbs said, and he urged his horse to the head of his small column, leaving his corporal with a questioning look on his smooth black face.

Chapter Eight

"Mama!" Peg's voice was filled with alarm.

Mac had been pretending to be asleep for nearly an hour, watching Peg through half-closed eyes while his head lolled from side to side in time with the jouncing covered wagon. Years of practice at Boston Latin School, with the nuns checking the dormitory each night, had made him an expert at feigning sleep. But he had grown tired of fooling Peg and had turned to her, eyes wide open, and stared at her until she noticed him and called her mother.

"Who are you?" Mac said. He could remember seeing this girl in the wagon next to the woman, but he didn't know her name.

"Mama!" Peg called again. "He's awake."

Mac sat up and looked around the swaying wagon. It was small and cramped, crammed with pieces of furniture, blankets, clothes, tools, assorted chests and valises stacked nearly to the curved metal struts supporting the taut canvas overhead. Peg was sitting in a small rocking chair, doubt and suspicion plain on her pretty face. Mac looked beyond her, through the opening at the front of the wagon, and saw Aaron walking beside the team, the reins in his hands. His wife was perched on the seat, arms folded over her swollen midsection.

"Are we going to Denver?" he yelled.

Cindy turned and smiled at him. Moving awkwardly with her protruding belly, she struggled into the back of the wagon. "Well, look who's sitting up to take notice. How're you feeling?" She opened one of the small chests and took out a round metal container. "I expect you're a little hungry right about now," she said, as she tried to pry the lid off the container.

Mac didn't answer, but she was right. He was starving. He felt like he hadn't eaten in days. Come to think of it, he probably hadn't. The last meal he remembered was beans and tortillas and two pieces of prickly pear pie. The thought of it nauseated him. Cindy finally got the can open and handed him a hardtack biscuit. He accepted it without comment and took a big bite. He had always hated hardtack, but this was the most delicious thing he had ever tasted in his life.

Cindy's smile faded, and her eyes narrowed. "You're welcome," she said, her voice cool.

Mac ignored her. *I've got more important things to think about than saying thank you,* he told himself as he finished the hardtack. "How long before we get to Denver?"

Cindy smiled again, but without warmth, and shook her head. "You might not have any manners," she said, putting the cover back on the can, "but I'll say this for you. Once you set your mind to something, you stick to it." She put the can away and opened a wicker basket and began to take out tin plates and eating utensils. She turned to Peg and said, "Help me with these dishes, sweetie; we'll be stopping to eat soon."

That's good news, Mac thought. *She didn't even offer me another hardtack.*

Peg took the plates and started putting knives and forks with them, and Cindy turned her attention to Mac again. "As for Denver, I'm afraid you'd better forget about it for a while. We'll try to get word to your family when we get to the fort."

Oh, no, Mac thought, cold fear clutching his chest, *not my uncle.* "I don't have a family," he said.

Cindy's brow wrinkled, and she gave him a suspicious look. "Then where were you going on the stage? And who is this Gus and Mushy you asked about?"

Mac was beginning to feel trapped. He had to tell her something. "I, ah, I was going to Benson to . . ." *Uh-oh, maybe I shouldn't tell her that.* "But I—I changed my mind."

"What's in Benson?" Cindy's eyes were accusing.

"Nothing. I, ah, I was just going there to—to see someone." *Drat! That was a dumb thing to say. Now how do I get out of this?*

"A relative?" Cindy persisted.

"Just someone." Mac's mind raced. "Could I have another hardtack, please? I'm awfully hungry."

Cindy chuckled and shook her head again. "You might as well tell me. Benson's a pretty small town, so I'll find out anyway."

Mac was angry with himself for mentioning Benson. Now he'd have to tell her; there was no way out. "I was going to see my uncle." Then he added quickly, "But I changed my mind."

"Well, you'll just have to change it back again." Cindy winced and shifted her position slightly. "Meanwhile, it might help if we knew your name."

"I'm J. Wentworth McAllister the third," Mac blurted, "and I demand that you . . ."

"The third what?" Peg asked, snickering, and she hid a grin behind her hand.

"Now, Peg," Cindy scolded gently, "be nice." But Mac noticed the woman couldn't help smiling herself. *I don't see what they find so funny,* he thought, and he glared at both mother and daughter. "Well, J. Wentworth McAllister the third," Cindy went on, "we could use a little help with the noon meal." She grunted as she moved back toward the front of the wagon. "As you can see, I'm a little slow getting around these days."

Outside, Aaron took off his hat and wiped his brow with his shirtsleeve. Cindy settled into the driver's seat and called out to him. "Is it about time to eat?"

Aaron gauged the position of the sun and nodded. "Any time now. And looks like we might have company," he said, pointing off to the right of the wagons.

Hobbs was approaching at a canter. As he drew near, he slowed his horse to a walk and rode alongside the Wry wagon, abreast of the driver's seat. He saluted Cindy and said, "How's our young millionaire doin'?"

"Awake and ornery," she replied. "I think he's hungry."

Hobbs smiled. "He must be feelin' better."

Aaron waved to Hobbs and handed the reins up to his wife. Then he yelled to the wagons behind him. "We'll stop here to eat and rest the stock. Be ready to move on in half an hour."

As Cindy reined the wagon to a halt, Peg thrust a stack of tin plates at Mac. "Help me carry these outside, please."

Mac stuffed his hands into his pockets. "Ha," he snorted, and he turned his back to her. "That's your job."

"Mama said you were supposed to help."

"That's women's work." Mac stretched out on the blankets and put his arms behind his head. "Let me know when lunch is ready."

"Mama!" Peg yelled. She poked her head through the

opening at the front of the wagon just as Aaron was helping Cindy down from the driver's seat. "Mama," Peg said again, "he won't help."

Aaron looked up at Peg. "You tell him if he don't help, he don't eat." Hobbs nodded in silent agreement.

"Can't you tell him?" Peg pleaded. "He acts like he's— like he's boss of the wagon or somethin'."

"Wait'll we get settled," Cindy told her. "I'll see to Mr. McAllister."

That'll be the day, Mac said to himself, and he moved so that he could lean his back against a small trunk and crossed his arms over his chest. Through the rear opening of the canvas he could see people stretching and yawning as they climbed down from their wagons. Some of them were already preparing food, and the sight of it made Mac's stomach grumble, and his mouth filled with saliva. Peg gave him a cold stare, then climbed over the tailgate and disappeared around the side of the wagon. Mac heard her say, "I told you he wouldn't help," just before Aaron's face appeared at the opening in the canvas.

He scowled at Mac. "Time to eat, young fella."

"Fine," Mac said, stretching his legs out farther and clasping his hands behind his head. "I'll have my lunch in here, please."

Aaron shook his head and grinned thinly. "You're a piece of work, I'll say that for ya."

Just then Hobbs joined Aaron at the rear of the wagon and put a hand on his shoulder. "I found him," he said. "He's my problem as much as yours." He glared at Mac, and when he spoke, his voice was quiet but menacing. "Kid, you got about two minutes to git your tail down here."

"Or what?" Mac said, suddenly a little afraid.

"You don't wanna find out," Hobbs said, and he and Aaron walked away, out of Mac's view.

Mac kept telling himself he didn't have to do anything he didn't want to, but after wondering for a moment what his father would have done in this situation, he decided that he was hungry enough to make a concession this once. He climbed over the tailgate and dropped to the ground. The Wrys and Hobbs were standing next to a narrow ledge that ran along the side of the wagon by the water barrel. Mac watched for a few minutes while Cindy cut thick slices from a plump loaf of bread and Peg set out the tin plates and utensils. The bread looked delicious, and Mac realized he was almost faint from hunger.

"Where do I wash?" he demanded.

Everyone turned in his direction, surprised looks on their faces. Hobbs was the first to find his voice. "Wash? What for? You ain't done nothin' yet to git dirty."

Peg covered a grin with her hand, and Hobbs went to Mac and took a firm grip on his shoulder. He steered him to the side of the wagon and pointed at a slab of dried meat wrapped up in oilcloth. "Here, cut us some of that smoked meat." He took the bowie knife out of the sheath at his belt and stropped it a few times on the side of his boot before handing it to Mac. "And be careful ya don't slice off a finger."

Mac, knife in hand, stood staring at the meat, reluctant to go near it.

"It won't bite," Hobbs said, and Peg giggled again.

Mac put his face down to the oilcloth and sniffed. As hungry as he was, the strong, greasy odor turned his stomach. He wrinkled up his nose and turned away. "What is it?" he said, nearly gagging.

"Ain't you ever seen smoked beef before?" Hobbs asked. Mac held his nose. "It stinks."

"Ya don't smell it, ya eat it."

"Yuck!" Mac stuck his tongue out.

"I'll grant ya," Hobbs said, "it don't exactly smell like fried chicken, but . . ."

"I'm not touching it," Mac declared. He threw the knife down on the ground and backed away from the wagon.

"We'll see about that," Hobbs said, and he started to unbuckle his belt.

Cindy put a hand on his arm. "Let me." Her voice was soft but firm. Hobbs shrugged, and she went to Mac's side and put an arm around his shoulders. "I want to explain something to you—ah—Mac."

In spite of Cindy's quiet tone, Mac felt threatened. There was something in her voice that reminded him of Sister Vera just before she was ready to explode. He had to set her straight, and right now. "My name's not Mac. It's . . ."

"I know what your name is," Cindy said sharply, "but I don't have time for J. Wentworth the third and all the rest, so let's just settle for Mac." She held him by both shoulders and stared deep into his eyes. "Look, I'm sorry you got separated from the folks on the stage. We'll do our best to contact your uncle as soon as we get to Fort Huachuca. But meanwhile you can make things a whole lot easier if you just follow a few simple rules."

Mac twisted away from her grasp. "My father said rules were for sheep."

"Then," Cindy shot back, her eyes snapping, "if you know what's good for you, you'd better learn to grow wool."

Mac felt his cheeks turn hot, and he glared at Peg as she hid her face behind her hands. He knew she was laughing at him again. And so was Hobbs. The big black man just stood there nodding, a half smile on his face.

"Ordinarily, I like little boys," Cindy continued, and Mac stretched himself to his fullest height. "The Good Lord willing, we might even have one of our own before long." She patted her belly, and Peg made a gagging sound and wrinkled up her face. "But right now, you do your share of work in this family, or you're going to wish that this man," she said, pointing to Hobbs, "had left you out there where he found you."

She took Mac by the collar of his shirt and marched him, stumbling and squirming, back to the wagon. "Now, pick that up," she said, and she forced him to retrieve the abandoned knife. Mac glared at her, and the heat rose in his cheeks again until even the tips of his ears felt warm. Cindy glared back at him, and for a moment her face was the face of Sister Vera.

"Preparing food is women's work," he said, his voice trembling with anger. He gave Cindy a hateful look, threw the knife into the dirt again, and stomped to the rear of the wagon, where he leaned against the wheel and crossed his arms defiantly. Aaron, Cindy, and Hobbs all exchanged dark, angry looks; nobody spoke. Peg picked up the knife, wiped it on her apron, and started to cut strips of meat.

After a long silence Hobbs said, "His belly ain't empty enough yet. He'll feel different come suppertime."

That's what you think, Mac said to himself. He was already starving. He began to wonder if maybe he should have cut the meat after all. It didn't really smell *that* bad. Out of the corner of his eye he saw Aaron and Cindy go to the water barrel and begin to ladle out water.

Hobbs joined them. "Look," he said, "we're gonna hafta

be movin' on. I—I'm sorry the kid's such a pain in the . . .
Well, I'm just sorry, that's all."

"What about the Indians?" Aaron said, a trace of concern in his voice.

"Looks like they cleared out," Hobbs replied. "At least
for now. Besides, we'll pick up their trail pretty quick. If
they head back this way, we'll be right behind 'em." Then
he retrieved his knife and went quickly to his horse,
mounted, and loped off toward where Levi and the troopers waited.

Cindy and Aaron followed him for a few steps and stood
watching as he rode away.

Peg was putting meat on the plates. Mac risked a glance
in her direction just as she looked up at him. He was about
to look away, but something in her face held his gaze. No
giggling and snickering now; her dark brown eyes looked
gentle, and for just an instant he thought he detected a flash
of sympathy, maybe even a hint of understanding.

"Don't you want something to eat?" she said quietly.

Mac didn't know what to say, didn't even know how he
really felt, and couldn't understand why he didn't just accept Peg's offer. But he just couldn't. So, shoulders sagging,
he turned and walked to the rear of the wagon.

There were tears on his cheeks.

Hobbs signaled to his men, and they reined to a stop behind
him. He dismounted and knelt to examine the faint impressions of horses' hooves in the clay soil. Most of the tracks
had been made by shoeless ponies, but a few imprints were
sharper and cut deeper into the hard ground. Hobbs figured
that the Indians who had made the tracks had probably stolen some shod animals, maybe even army horses.

Levi dismounted and squatted beside him. "Think those belong to Geronimo, Sarge?"

"Could be."

"Then what're we waitin' for?" Levi's eyes shone with excitement. He pointed to a small adobe house set in a shallow valley less than a half mile in the distance. The house was partially surrounded by a stone fence, and a corral held a half dozen horses, about evenly split between saddle horses and work animals. "Looks like he mighta been headin' for that ranch down there."

"Even if it was Geronimo who made these tracks," Hobbs said, "ain't likely he'd still be holed up at that ranch—if he was ever there. And we ain't gonna catch up with him if he don't wanna be caught up with." He looked back at his men. The troopers' blue uniforms were mottled with dust, and their mounts were lathered with sweat. "Besides, our horses are near dead."

"But what if he gets away?" Levi protested.

"Our job's to follow him, remember? Not catch him." Hobbs swung up into his saddle, and Levi, looking a little pouty, followed suit. "Let's just ride down there," Hobbs said, "and see if that rancher'll let us water our horses and maybe rest 'em up for a few hours."

He ignored Levi's pout and commanded his squad into motion.

Chapter Nine

The men are buryin' 'em around back," Levi said.

He had come into the main room of the adobe ranch house just as Hobbs was thumbing through a scuffed, hardcover ledger by the light of a kerosene lantern. The yellowed pages contained notations in a scrawled handwriting that described the sales of cattle, the purchase of horses, expenses for feed and grain, and assorted debits and credits. Near the back of the book Hobbs found a folded piece of paper. He opened it and started to read.

"Find out who they were?" Levi asked.

Hobbs finished reading and handed him the paper. Levi studied it for a minute, his face screwed up in concentration.

Then, with a solemn look, he shook his head and handed it back.

"Can't ya read?" Hobbs said harshly, knowing the answer to his question.

"Slaves wasn't allowed, remember?"

"We ain't been slaves for more'n ten years," Hobbs growled. He didn't really know why, but it bothered him that Levi couldn't read. He liked his young corporal, yet sometimes he thought he was a little too interested in just wanting to do things that were fun—or things he thought would be fun, like fighting Indians. *He'll find out that's no kinda fun,*

Hobbs thought. Also it bothered him that Levi, and several other young black men he knew, had never taken time to learn to read after they became free men. To Hobbs, that kind of lack of ambition reflected badly on all men of color. *We gotta be better than that,* he told himself.

"Time ya learned," he said when Levi handed back the paper. Hobbs folded it up and tucked it into an inside jacket pocket. "According to this," he said, tapping a spot over the pocket, "their name was McAllister." Then he turned away and stepped through the splintered frame where the door had once hung and out into the rapidly descending darkness.

Levi followed him and pointed to the corral. "Why do ya think they left the horses?"

Hobbs shrugged. "If I had to guess, I'd say they probably knew we were gettin' close and figgered the extra animals would slow 'em down." He walked to where the squad's horses were feeding next to the watering trough and began to unsaddle his mount. "We'll camp here tonight. When the men are done buryin', post a couple guards, and . . ."

"I know, I know," Levi said, and he heaved a sigh. "And make a cold camp."

Hobbs couldn't help but chuckle. "They can have a hot meal if they want," he said. "Have 'em cook inside."

Levi's smile lit up the night. And as he wheeled and ran toward the back of the house, Hobbs wondered if he was being too hard on him. After all, he was just a kid. He had a lot of years ahead of him to learn to read—and to fight Indians.

Aaron finished the last of his coffee and threw the dregs, hissing and steaming, into the dwindling flames of the cook fire. Then he dunked his mug in the bucket Peg was using to wash the dirty dishes from their supper. From where she was drying plates and storing them in a hamper, Cindy looked up, past Aaron, and her eyes narrowed to a cold squint.

Aaron followed her gaze and saw Loren Pike. Rifle in hand, he was making his way past the other cook fires and through the families clustered around them in the darkness. "Looks like company's comin'," he said, and he gave a short, mirthless laugh as he glanced at his wife.

Cindy's look grew darker in the pale glow from the fire. "I just burned the welcome mat." She slammed the lid on the dish hamper, took Peg by the elbow, and headed for their wagon as Pike stepped into the circle of flickering light.

"This is crazy, Wry," Pike hissed. He darted nervous glances into the darkness beyond the flames. "We shoulda put them fires out before dark."

"The Indians already know we're here, Pike. If they mean to do us harm, they know where to find us." Aaron picked up the bucket of dishwater and, with Pike trailing after him, started toward the perimeter of the circled wagons.

"Whatta you know about Indians?" Pike demanded. "You ain't nothin' but a storekeeper."

"I never claimed to be anything else." Aaron dumped the water, not really caring when it seemed to accidentally splash on Pike.

"All the same," Pike whined as they turned back toward the cook fire, "I think we're takin' a big chance settin' here like candles in a shootin' gallery."

Aaron didn't respond. Instead, he hung the empty bucket on a hook on the wagon.

Pike fidgeted with his rifle, and worry lines creased his

forehead. "Well, I'm puttin' mine out," he said, and headed quickly back the way he'd come toward his own wagon.

Cindy and Peg stepped out of the shadows and stood by Aaron. They watched as Pike began gesturing wildly at his wife; although they couldn't make out what he was saying, Liz scampered to gather up the supper utensils while her husband kicked dirt over the remnants of his cook fire.

The long, dancing shadows cast by the few remaining fires within the circle of wagons made Aaron suddenly gloomy, and he felt an uneasiness he couldn't explain. Though the night was warm, he felt a chill and put an arm around Cindy's shoulders. His voice was little more than a whisper when he said, "Where's Mac?"

"He's in the wagon," Cindy replied. "Where he's been all day."

"Good," Peg chimed in.

Aaron smiled but didn't feel amused; and, though he wasn't sure why, he felt his uneasiness mounting. "I'll just take a look," he said, and he ambled toward the rear of his wagon. He peered through the opening in the canvas, and as his eyes became adjusted to the dim light, he could make out Mac leaning against a keg, his hands clasped behind his head, his legs stretched out in front of him.

Aaron felt relieved. "Ain't you gettin' a little hungry?"

"I've gone a lot longer than this without eating," Mac replied sourly, but Aaron detected a note of uncertainty in his tone that made the boast somehow less than convincing.

"Well," he said, determined to penetrate Mac's wall of rebelliousness, "that may be, but there's no need for it this time. All you gotta do is help out a little with the—"

"I told you," Mac interrupted, his voice more defiant, "I don't do women's work."

Aaron's anger flared. He felt awkward, embarrassed that his gesture of kindness was so quickly rebuffed by this ten-year-old ingrate, this—this brat. "Suit yourself," he snapped. "No work, no food." He turned away from the wagon and stomped back toward the cook fire.

"Wait!" Mac's voice was plaintive now. Aaron paused, then took a few steps back toward the wagon, to where Mac's face was a white blur in the dark opening in the canvas. "Wait," he said again, his voice trembling. "Maybe I . . . Maybe I could . . ."

"Pa!" The call was more like a scream, filled with panic and choking off Mac's words. Peg dashed out of the darkness and ran to Aaron, clutching at his arm. "Pa!" she said again, "come quick! It's Mama—she's real bad."

Pike lit a kerosene lantern, turned it low, and hung it just inside the tailgate of his wagon. He watched as his wife struggled in the feeble light to clean up the last of the supper dishes. She drew water in a pail and lugged it to the back of the wagon, and for the third time since returning from his conversation with Aaron, Pike checked the load in his rifle.

"Can't you give me a hand instead of messin' with that gun?" Liz said between grunts as she shifted the pail from one hand to the other.

"I don't trust Wry to know what he's talkin' about," Pike said. "I wanna be ready if them sneakin' Indians come back." He stopped caressing his rifle and grinned at his wife. "Besides, I'll hire a maid for ya when we get to California."

"What're ya gonna use for money?" She set the pail down and brushed a wisp of stringy hair back from her forehead.

"Now, don't start that again," Pike ordered. He watched Liz try to rub the stiffness out of her back and wondered what he had ever seen in her in the first place. *God knows, she's lost whatever looks she had, and she ain't got enough meat on her to do any real work. If it wasn't for the property . . .* Then he said, "We're man and wife, remember?"

"Don't remind me."

"What's yours is mine. I can get a pretty penny for that land your uncle left ya."

"Don't count on it," Liz snarled. Pinpoints of yellow light from the lantern reflected in her eyes, and Pike thought she looked like some kind of scared, hateful animal. Then she heaved a deep sigh, and her voice sounded weary when she said, "I'll settle for just gettin' to California." She picked up the pail again and hoisted it into the back of the wagon.

Pike was about to put out the lantern when he caught sight of a movement in the shadows. His gut tightened, and his hands clutched the rifle closer to his body just as Aaron stepped into the pale light. "Well, look who's here," Pike said, and he let out a deep breath. "What's eatin' you, storekeeper?"

Aaron looked haggard, his face drawn. "My wife's just taken a bad turn, and I'm lookin' for someone to take the McAllister boy off my hands till we get to Fort Huachuca."

"Keep lookin'," Pike said, and he snickered at Aaron's pained look.

"Now, just a minute, Pike."

"Sorry, Wry," Pike said, enjoying Aaron's discomfort.

"But you're the only family that's got room."

"Forget it." Pike's voice was harsh. He was annoyed that Aaron would even suggest that Mac ride with them. "Whatta ya take me for, a nursemaid?" Aaron's eyes narrowed, and though the light was poor, Pike could see his jaw muscles flexing. Then, just as Aaron turned and started back into the darkness, Pike felt a hand on his arm.

"Don't be a fool," Liz whispered. "I can use the help. And if it turns out the boy really does have money . . ."

That was all Pike had to hear. "Wry!"

"Aaron, wait!" Liz chimed in.

Aaron stopped and walked slowly back to the wagon. "Maybe I been a little hard on the kid," Pike began. "He can ride with us." The anger in Aaron's face of a moment before melted into a look of suspicion. Pike put an arm around his wife's waist. "Besides, you said the missus here could use a hand."

Aaron's brow furrowed, and he eyed Pike coolly. "Now, hold on. You make it sound like I'm sellin' a bonded servant. I just want someone to keep an eye on him for a few days."

Liz smiled sweetly and looked up at her husband. "We'll treat him like one of the family," she cooed. "Won't we, dear?"

"Sure," Pike said. "Like one o' the family."

Aaron kneaded his beard and paused for what seemed like a long time before he answered. "Ah . . . I . . . I don't know. Maybe I was too quick. Maybe . . ."

"C'mon, Wry," Pike said, grinning. "We'll take real good care o' the kid."

"How could you?" Cindy's accusing tone stung Aaron like the bite of a whip. She stood facing him, feet planted apart, hands on her hips, and her eyes snapping.

"Because you ain't up to takin' care of another youngster right now," he argued. "Especially one like Mac."

"Fiddlesticks." Cindy cupped her hands under her unborn child. "I just had a few pains, that's all." She went to where Peg was setting out several pans of soda bread to cool beside the dying embers of the cook fire. Mother and daughter covered the plump loaves with rectangles of white cloth.

Aaron picked up the rifle leaning against the wagon. "Yeah, but it's too early for pains like that. And these ain't the first ones you've had."

Cindy straightened and stood rubbing the small of her back with both hands. "I'll be worried sick about him," she said, her tone still angry. "Even if he is a pest." Peg glanced at her but said nothing.

"Maybe Pike's just what Mac needs to cure his stubborn streak," Aaron persisted, as he checked his rifle and made sure it was fully loaded, then went to where Peg was covering the last loaf of bread. "Besides, we can look in on him every day." He caressed Peg's head and brushed his lips against her hair before he turned to look at Cindy. "You two had better get some sleep," he said gently, hoping to find a softening in his wife's eyes. But there was no such reprieve.

He squatted and reached for one of the loaves of bread. Moving swiftly despite her bulk, Cindy slapped his hand away. "Wait till it cools," she snapped.

Aaron knew it would do no good to argue; he knew that Cindy's anger, like the bread, would cool in its own good time. He sighed and stood up, cradling the rifle in the crook of his arm. "I got first lookout," he said, and he sauntered toward the deep blackness beyond the circle of wagons.

Peg parted the canvas and peeked out, her eyes trying to penetrate the darkness that enveloped the circled wagons. The cook fire was reduced to a faintly glowing ash, and she held her breath and listened, but there were only the soft sounds of snoring and the occasional nickering of a horse. She climbed silently over the tailgate and, clutching her nightgown close to her neck against the chill of the desert night, padded to where the pans of bread were still set out neatly on the ground. She felt one of the loaves, and it was cool. She turned back the cloth cover and shook the bread out of its pan and, with a quick glance back toward the wagon, slipped into the night.

Peg's eyes became accustomed to the dark in the few minutes it took her to reach the rear of the Pike wagon. Standing on tiptoe, she reached over the tailgate, turned back a small triangle of canvas, and strained to see into the dark interior. Her gaze followed the sound of loud snoring, and she could just make out the form of Loren Pike. He was flat on his back, mouth open. Liz was asleep next to him, her head half-buried under a blanket. Mac lay apart from them, arms folded behind his head, but Peg couldn't tell if he was asleep or awake.

"Pssst!"

Mac raised himself up on one elbow. "Who is it?"

"Shh, come here."

He squirmed to the back of the wagon, and his eyes widened when he recognized Peg. "What are you . . . ?"

"Shh," Peg cautioned again. "Whisper. I brought you something to eat." She held up the loaf of bread where Mac could see it, and its fragrance filled the back of the wagon.

"I don't need anything to eat," Mac grumbled. "Especially from a girl."

"Don't be dumb," Peg told him.

Mac sniffed, then sniffed again. Peg backed away from the wagon and waited. Mac sniffed once more, then climbed to the ground, where Peg led him to the deeper shadows and handed him the bread.

"I thought you didn't like me," he said before he tore off a chunk of bread and stuffed it into his mouth.

"I don't," Peg informed him. "I feel sorry for you."

"You don't feel sorry for people you don't like," Mac said, his words nearly lost in his frantic chewing.

"I'd feel sorry for anybody who had to ride with Mr. Pike." Peg was secretly glad she had a good excuse for bringing Mac the bread. She really did feel sorry for him, but more than that she found herself starting to like him—in spite of his rudeness and spoiled, bossy ways. She was suddenly embarrassed, certain that Mac could read her innermost thoughts; she was glad it was dark, because she was sure she was blushing.

Mac tore at the bread savagely, and his cheeks ballooned as he forced it into his mouth. Peg thought he looked like a chipmunk, but a cute one. Then, feeling more embarrassed than ever, she turned and ran, ignoring Mac's garbled pleas for her to come back.

Chapter Ten

The first streaks of a new day spread like pink ribbons across the eastern rim of the desert, washing out the pin-points of starlight that dotted the dark sky. Geronimo squatted on his haunches, listening to the muffled snores coming from the wagons and an occasional sigh from the horses that were drowsing where they stood. The light was just enough for him to make out the lone guard who plodded around the outer edge of the circled wagon train. As he walked, the guard yawned and hunched his shoulders in the pre-dawn chill.

Geronimo stood up and, without a sound, moved to where a half dozen Apaches waited by their horses some twenty or thirty yards away. With no need to speak, he made a sign to Sanchez and motioned toward the wagons. Sanchez nodded and melted into the darkness. In a few seconds a thud and a grunt from the shadows confirmed that the guard had been disposed of.

Leading their horses, the Apaches followed Geronimo to where Sanchez waited. Then, making a sign for quiet, he led them single file as they walked their horses through a gap between the wagons. The false dawn spread a gray light over the circle of dead fires and the scattered cooking utensils that had been left out from the previous night's meals. Geronimo pointed to a half dozen pans of bread set beside a fire that had grown cold under a cooking pot still suspended from a tripod. He crouched by the pans, tossed aside their cloth covers, and began handing loaves to the men squatting behind him. Each man in turn ripped off a share of bread and fell to eating quickly and eagerly. Geronimo knew their bellies were empty, and he joined them in savoring the fresh, crusty treat. Hunting had been poor of late; there had been little time for it with the black soldiers on their trail. *It is difficult to hunt* and *run,* Geronimo thought.

"This time we take the horses," Sanchez whispered between bites of bread.

Geronimo looked at the rapidly brightening sky. Now worry began to gnaw at his belly along with the hunger. He wished they had come upon the wagon train earlier, while it was still dark.

He finally answered Sanchez. "Those are work horses."

"Then we eat them," Sanchez hissed.

Geronimo stared at the young brave and shook his head. He knew Sanchez was right; they certainly could use the horses for food, but now was not the time. The sun was nearly up, and the white men in the wagons would soon be awake. Sanchez was about to protest when another brave put a hand on Geronimo's arm and pointed to the east, where a swirl of dust rose on the distant horizon, barely visible in the long streaks of sunlight breaking over the mountains.

The black soldiers! Geronimo felt the familiar surge of excitement, but it was tainted now with a hint of weariness as he stuffed the last piece of bread into his mouth. These days they didn't even have time to eat. He motioned for his men to mount up, but as he started for his own horse, Sanchez moved to block his way.

"I will not be denied this time," he growled. "I say we take the horses."

Geronimo shook his head and started around the young brave. Again Sanchez moved to block him but lost his footing and stumbled against the cooking tripod. Both pot and tripod clanged into the dirt, the noise loud in the silent encampment. The Apaches froze for an instant, their dark eyes darting from wagon to wagon; then they swung up onto their waiting ponies.

From horseback, Geronimo saw the face of a startled white man appear at the opening in the back of a wagon. He was partially hidden by the canvas flap, and when he saw Geronimo, his beady eyes widened like an owl's, round and staring. Geronimo held his gaze for a moment, then turned at the sound of rifles being cocked behind him. Some of his band raised their weapons, ready to fire.

"No!" Geronimo shouted. "We came only for food."

Sanchez ignored the order. He put his rifle to his shoulder and took aim at the man in the wagon. Geronimo wheeled his horse and lunged, knocking the weapon to one side, but not in time to prevent Sanchez from firing, and the crack of the rifle shattered the early-dawn quiet.

Mac wondered if he had been dreaming. Was that a gunshot? Then he heard a woman scream, and he bolted upright, his heart racing. He saw Loren Pike peering out through the canvas flap at the back of the wagon. Then the man jumped back, his face drawn and white, his eyes bulging.

"Apaches!" Pike barked, an edge of fear in his voice. He turned for his rifle just as Liz, near panic, struggled up from her blankets and clutched at his arm.

"What is it?" she demanded. "Apaches where?"

Pike pushed her away, cocked his weapon, returned to the back of the wagon, and parted the canvas flap a few inches. "I told Wry to put them fires out last night."

Mac moved to a position where he could get a glimpse of what was happening outside. All he could see was about a half dozen mounted Indians. Their ponies were prancing and snorting, ears pricked up and nostrils flaring. Except for the one who seemed to be in charge, they were waving their rifles and war lances and motioning toward Pike's wagon.

"They'll kill us all!" Liz cried, blubbering and sobbing as she again clung to her husband's arm.

"Not hardly," Pike said. He shoved her aside and poked his rifle through the opening in the canvas. "A few thievin' Apaches ain't gonna keep me from gettin' to California."

Mac, his heart still pounding, edged closer to Pike to get a better view. The Apache leader was shaking his fist at a young brave who was pointing his rifle at Pike and threatening to shoot. The two Indians glared at each other and growled a few words that Mac couldn't understand, but he knew they were arguing. It looked like the older Apache wanted the younger one to follow the other Indians who were now beginning to file out of the circle of wagons.

Eyes burning, the scowling brave lowered his rifle and was turning his horse just as Pike took aim at one of the retreating Indians.

"No!" Mac yelled. "They're leaving!"

"Shut yer mouth," Pike ordered, and his finger whitened around the trigger. Mac lunged for his arm just as the sound of the rifle blast filled the wagon, and the smell of exploded gunpowder burned his nose and made his eyes water. Through the blur of tears, he saw a young Indian, blood streaming down his face, slump over his horse's neck. The Apache leader moved quickly to his side and caught him before he could fall to the ground. The other Indians stopped and turned toward Pike's wagon. The anger that burned in their eyes made Mac shiver.

Liz screamed, then blubbered, "Oh, my God! Now they'll kill us all for sure."

"Shut up," Pike barked through clenched teeth. His face was ashen, and his hands trembled when he pulled back from the opening in the canvas. Just then the young brave who had been arguing with the Apache chief bolted to the wagon and, with a frightening shriek, pulled back the canvas. Liz screamed again, and the Apache, his face a mask of hate and his black eyes burning holes into Pike, aimed his rifle. Pike, eyes threatening to leave their sockets and spittle dripping from his mouth, threw up his hands in a useless gesture of defense and began to babble meaningless words. Liz collapsed onto the wagon bed in a quivering mound of fear.

Realizing he had been holding his breath, Mac let out a lungful of air just as the Apache leader rode up, grumbled a few words to the younger man, and pointed to the cloud of dust beyond the perimeter of the wagon train. Then they both wheeled their horses and picked their way through an opening between the wagons to where the other Indians waited.

Now a few men from the train, rifles in hand, ventured cautiously into the circular compound. Talking all at once and waving their arms, they converged on Pike's wagon. One of them pointed toward the retreating Indians. "Look!"

The defiant young Apache had broken from the group and, with another shriek that turned Mac's heart cold, charged back into the circle of wagons. The small knot of men, fear plain on their faces, stood and gaped as he skidded to a stop at Pike's wagon. The Indian threw aside the canvas, reached inside, and grabbed Liz by the hair. She screamed hysterically while Pike cowered as deeply as he could into the depths of the wagon. Mac, heart racing, was frozen by the violence as the Apache pulled Liz, babbling, struggling, and screaming, out of the wagon and threw her across his horse in front of him.

Mac waited for the men from the other wagons to do something, but they just stared, their mouths hanging open. Liz lay limp across the Apache's horse, sobbing but not moving, her eyes closed. The young Indian, his coppery face twisted in a snarl, spat out a few words in Apache dialect while he waved his rifle over his head. Then, with a jerk on the reins that caused his horse to rear, he spun around and, with a final shriek, raced after his departing companions.

Pike was the first to recover. He emerged from deep in his wagon, pushed Mac aside, and peered over the tailgate at the rapidly disappearing Indians; then he turned to the small knot of men who had come alive and were grumbling and gesturing among themselves.

"What'd he say?" Pike demanded. "Anyone here understand that red devil? Anyone know Apache?"

A grizzled man in overalls stepped forward. "I think he said somethin' about killin' her if that wounded Indian dies."

Mac clung to the tailgate as Pike climbed down from the wagon and elbowed his way through the crowd of men, then stopped when he saw Aaron approaching. "About time ya showed up," he said, sneering. "I suppose ya been hidin' in your wagon."

Aaron's face was flushed behind his beard. "Just so hap-

pens I got a sick wife that needed tendin' to. But I could
see enough to know what was happenin', and what I want
to know is why you fired that shot. That was an idiot thing
to do."

"Yeah," said the man in overalls, shaking his fist. "You
coulda got us all killed." Other voices from the crowd
echoed agreement, and the men growled their displeasure
as they pressed closer, enclosing Pike in a circle of bodies.
Pike's eyes flitted from face to face in a crowd that now,
along with more men, included several women and children,
and he backed toward the protection of his wagon. Then he
glared at Mac.

"He's the one that done it."

Mac couldn't believe what he was hearing. "That's not
true," he protested. "I didn't do—"

"I never intended to shoot," Pike cut in, pointing a skinny,
accusing finger at Mac. "He hit my arm, and—"

"He ought to be whipped good," one of the men interrupted, followed by shouts of agreement from the crowd.

"Now, just hang on," Aaron said, pushing his way toward
Pike. "Let's not have any talk about anyone bein' whipped
till we know who did what."

"What about my wife?" Pike demanded. "Don't anyone
care about her? I can't go to California without my wife!"

The man in overalls snorted. "We're just lucky them Indians ran off."

"Luck had nothin' to do with it," Aaron told him, and he
pointed beyond the wagons. All eyes turned toward the rising sun, where a squad of cavalry was less then a few hundred yards away, riding full tilt for the wagons. The troopers
had their weapons drawn, and their straining horses glistened with sweat. A cheer went up from the crowd, and they

surged beyond the circle of wagons to greet the approaching soldiers. Mac climbed down from Pike's wagon and followed them.

Sergeant Hobbs was at the head of the advancing column. He reined his horse to a stop at the edge of the crowd, and his men, equipment clanging, came to a halt behind him, enveloping the waiting wagoneers in a layer of dust. He turned to Levi and pointed beyond the wagons in the direction that marked the trail of the departing Indians. "Take some men and keep them Apaches in sight. I'll catch up with ya later. After I see what's goin' on here."

Levi selected five men and led them at a gallop away from the wagons as Hobbs climbed down from his saddle. "The rest of you men, spread out," he said to the remaining troopers, "and keep your eyes open." The soldiers dispersed and took up positions around the wagon train.

Aaron stepped out of the crowd and held out his hand. "I like your timing, Sergeant," he said, smiling.

"A little too close to suit me," Hobbs said. He didn't return Aaron's smile. "I promised to keep an eye on them Apaches for ya, but I let 'em get too far ahead of me. It won't happen again."

Aaron and Hobbs shook hands while the crowd pressed closer, their smiling faces showing a mixture of relief and gratitude. All except Pike; his face was clouded in a dark scowl. He forced his way out of the crowd and stood face-to-face with Hobbs, sneering.

"They got my wife. What're ya gonna do about it?"

Hobbs gave him a long look before he said, "Everything we can." Then he turned back to Aaron. "Anyone hurt? We heard shots."

"That was the kid's fault," Pike said, glancing quickly at

the faces in the crowd until his gaze came to rest on Mac. "I'm sorry I ever agreed to let him ride in my wagon." Mac felt his face grow warm, but he stared back at Pike, determined not to be intimidated. His father had always told him to never back down from a man who would lie. But he was surprised when Pike suddenly grabbed him by the arm and dragged him to the center of the crowd. "You shoulda left him out in the desert where ya found him," he said to Hobbs.

"If I knew he'd be ridin' with you," Hobbs answered, "I just mighta done that."

Pike's bony fingers sank into Mac's arm, and Mac tried to twist away, but that just made Pike squeeze harder. Hobbs glared and took a menacing step in his direction, and Pike let Mac go and stumbled backward into the crowd. Then Hobbs turned his gaze on Mac. Mac thought he saw a flicker of sympathy in the black soldier's eyes, but before he could be sure, he felt a gentle hand on his shoulder. He looked around as Cindy moved to his side, drawing him close. Mac felt suddenly safe, comforted by the gentle pressure of her swollen belly against him. Peg joined them, and Cindy pulled her close as well and stood with an arm around each of them.

Pike cast a hateful look at Cindy, then slunk back toward his wagon, where he continued to eye her warily.

Hobbs stepped to the center of the circle of people and said, "You folks better git movin' soon as ya can."

Pike squared his shoulders and started toward Hobbs but stopped several feet away, as though not sure how close he should get to the large black man. His lips peeled back from his teeth, and his eyes filled with a mixture of loathing and fear. He reminded Mac of a cornered rat. "I don't need your kind tellin' me what to do," he snarled. "What about my wife? That's all I wanna hear from you. What're ya doin' about her?"

"*My kind* is out there right now followin' her," Hobbs spat back. His eyes were dark, glowing coals, and Pike seemed to wither under their fierce glare.

"What'll happen to her, Sergeant?" Aaron asked.

"Lord only knows," Hobbs said, turning away from Pike, and his look softened. "But you can't do her no good waitin' around here. You'd best git to Fort Huachuca and tell Cap'n Horner what happened."

As Hobbs started away, he motioned for Aaron to follow him. They stopped by Hobbs' horse and stood for a moment talking softly, privately. Hobbs took a folded paper out of an inside jacket pocket and handed it to Aaron. As he read it, Aaron's eyes widened, and he cast a quick look at Mac, then turned his attention back to the paper. He finished reading and with another glance at Mac folded the paper, put it in a shirt pocket, then went back to talking with Hobbs.

Mac could only wonder what their conversation was about, but whatever it was, from the look on Aaron's face it wasn't likely to be good news. Aaron shook hands with Hobbs and watched as he swung up into his saddle and yelled for his troopers to reassemble. Then, as the cavalrymen headed for the open desert following the direction Levi had taken, Aaron made his way slowly back to the throng still milling around Pike's wagon.

"All right, everybody, back to your wagons. We need to get goin' as soon as we can." Appearing eager to get under way, the crowd melted quickly toward their animals and began to hitch up their teams.

Only Pike stayed behind. "You can't go without my wife, Wry."

"You heard the sergeant," Aaron said. "The soldiers are doin' all they can for her. Right now I got the rest of these people to worry about."

Pike looked like he was going to say something else but changed his mind. He gave Mac a hateful stare, then, grumbling, stalked toward his hobbled horses.

Aaron watched him for a moment before he walked slowly to where Cindy waited with Mac and Peg. His brow was furrowed and his mouth set in a straight line that drew his chin whiskers up to his mustache. Mac squeezed closer to Cindy, trying to control the uneasy feeling that was beginning to creep into his gut.

"I'm sorry," Cindy said firmly before Aaron had a chance to speak, "but we can't let this boy stay with Pike. We'll just have to put up with him . . ." She pulled Mac closer. "I mean, take care of him a while longer."

Aaron handed her the paper Hobbs had given him. "Maybe longer than you think." Cindy took the paper but didn't look at it; instead she questioned Aaron with her eyes, eyebrows raised.

"It's a telegraph message," he said quietly, and he glanced from Cindy to Mac and back again. "Hobbs found it a day or so ago. The Indians . . ." He glanced at Mac again. "The Indians killed a rancher and his wife." Aaron paused and let out a big breath. "The man's name was . . . His name was McAllister."

Cindy hugged Mac with both arms. "Oh, Mac, I'm sorry. So sorry."

Mac felt only relief. Now that his uncle was dead, he was sure he would be able to go back to Boston as soon as possible. The uneasiness of minutes before vanished.

Chapter Eleven

Hobbs decided his horse didn't need any help from him to pick its way through the rocks and boulders strewn about the floor of the canyon they were riding into. He turned his attention instead to the steep limestone walls on either side of him and his men, rising up to the high mesas above. He knew this was not a good position to be in, especially in hostile country. But it was where Levi's trail had led. *So where is he?* Hobbs wondered. He and his half of the squad had been riding hard; they should have caught up with him by now.

Only the sharp click of horses' hooves, echoing off the stone spires lining the canyon, broke the unnatural stillness. There was no sound of birds, no wind moving, not even a breeze to stir the air in this rocky furnace. Hobbs eyed the way ahead, searching for some sign that Levi was close at hand. Tracking over the rocky terrain was difficult, with only an occasional overturned or scuffed stone to indicate that other horses—shod horses—had passed this way. He turned in his saddle and looked back at the men. They, too, were feeling the uneasiness. Their wide eyes were round white circles in their glistening black faces, and they shifted their gaze constantly as they searched the rock formations high overhead.

The man nearest Hobbs pointed, his face pinched as though he had felt a sudden pain. "Look, Sergeant!" Hobbs followed his line of sight, and now he, too, felt the pain he had seen in the other man's eyes. They had found Levi.

Hobbs' hand shot up in a signal to halt. He scanned the ridges high overhead, and his heartbeat quickened, and, under his wool tunic, sweat trickled down his rib cage. He could see no actual signs of danger, but his instincts, and his experience, told him that he and his men were not alone. Then he turned his attention to the scene ahead. The canyon narrowed into a dry ravine that was strewn with the bodies of Levi and his men, bloodied, lying at grotesque angles, most of them stripped naked. Their horses were nowhere to be seen.

"Looks like Levi got his fight," Hobbs whispered, and a heavy sadness settled around his shoulders. But his melancholy was cut short by a series of piercing screams that echoed across the canyon, and a dozen mounted Apaches appeared at a turn in the ravine. With long black hair streaming and their weapons raised overhead, they thundered up the canyon.

"Dismount! Dismount!" Hobbs yelled as he sprang from his saddle. "But hang on to your horses."

His men tumbled from their mounts and scrambled for whatever protection they could find among the boulders scattered along the ravine. Following Hobbs' lead, they pulled their horses to the ground and took up firing positions behind them.

A few troopers snapped off hasty, ineffective shots at the approaching Indians. "Hold yer fire till they git closer!" Hobbs roared, as slugs from the Apache rifles began to zip and zing and kick up plumes of dirt around the waiting soldiers.

"Hold it," Hobbs said calmly as the charging riders drew closer. "Hold it. Steady." The growing sound of clattering hooves and wild screams filled the narrow ravine with a torrent of ear-shattering noise. The Apaches swept past in an awesome display of horsemanship, controlling their horses with their knees as they fired at a gallop.

"Now!" Hobbs yelled, above the din of the attack.

He and his men returned fire. The crack and thump of rifles and revolvers bounced from wall to wall in the canyon until it was impossible to tell real weapons fire from the echoes. Now the air was filled with the acrid stench of exploded gunpowder mixed with the sour smell of horses' sweat. Hobbs tracked a racing Apache, squeezed the trigger of his Winchester, and the Indian flipped backward out of his saddle, spinning slowly in midair before landing in his horse's tracks.

In the smoke and the stink and the noise, Hobbs could no longer be sure if his shots found their marks. The speed and skill of the attacking Indians made them hard targets. The trooper next to him suddenly rolled over and simply lay with his arms outstretched at his sides, as though asleep, except that his eyes were open, staring at nothing. Another soldier rose to his knees, hands covering the bloody mass that once was his face, and slumped over his horse and lay still. And as the last of the Indians raced past, one of the stragglers sagged in his saddle, struggled to stay upright, then slid to the ground and rolled over several times while his companions retreated to the protection of the opposite end of the ravine.

Then silence, as deep and penetrating as the clamor of seconds before, hung over the canyon. In the fading, dust-filled light of early evening, the troopers reloaded their weapons while darting quick looks at one another and at Hobbs, as though looking for reassurance or salvation.

"You're firin' wild," Hobbs said, his voice sounding too loud in the eerie quiet. "Take your time," he added while he stuffed more shells into the loading port on his rifle. "Hit what ya aim at."

"Think they'll be back, Sarge?" a young trooper asked in a voice laced with fear. "I think we picked off a couple of 'em."

"Here they come!" another soldier yelled before Hobbs could answer, and again screeching and thundering hoofbeats reverberated off the canyon walls.

"Wait for 'em," Hobbs said calmly, while he drew a bead on the lead Indian rider. He fired, and the horseman went down; then another soldier slumped over his horse, twitched once, and lay still. The Indians swept past in a repeat of the first charge, and when the noise and dust once again settled, only Hobbs and two troopers were left alive.

Hobbs could feel the two sets of frightened eyes boring into him as if they had weight and substance. "I'm just about outa catridges, Sarge," one man whispered, his voice hoarse and trembling.

Hobbs pointed to the dead troopers. "See what they got left." But before the man could move, the Apaches mounted their third attack. Hobbs found himself ignoring his own advice and fired as rapidly as he could at the advancing riders; he was only able to sneak a sideways glance as the last two troopers fell at nearly the same moment.

Then, in the midst of Apache screams and gunfire, Hobbs felt, as much as heard, the click of metal on metal as the hammer of his Winchester fell on an empty chamber.

Liz Pike struggled to no avail against the band of rawhide that bound a rag tightly around her mouth. Even as she grunted and strained, she knew that the Apache who held her in front of him on his horse was not going to loosen it. What she couldn't figure out was why he had brought her to the top of this mesa that overlooked the narrow canyon below.

The Apache held her tightly by the hair and turned her head so she was forced to look at him. He pointed at his eyes with the first two fingers of one hand and then pointed to the ravine below. Liz knew he wanted her to look, and what she saw startled her. From her vantage point, she could see what she guessed was about a dozen Apaches on horseback, sitting motionless as though they were waiting for something. Then she saw the mounted soldiers. Hobbs, the black sergeant she had seen at the wagon train, was leading them, and they entered the ravine slowly, their eyes constantly searching the tops of the steep walls that contained them.

The waiting Apaches were hidden from the soldiers by a sharp bend in the ravine, and now Liz realized what was happening. For her it was like watching a nightmare unfold. Men were going to be killed right before her eyes, and she was powerless to do anything about it. She shivered and tried to turn her head away, but her captor tightened his grip on her hair and forced her to continue watching.

The soldiers were stopped now, talking and gesturing toward something ahead of them. For the first time Liz noticed the bodies, lying black and naked amid the rocks and boulders on the floor of the ravine. She glimpsed some movement out of the corner of her eye and turned in time to see the waiting Apaches prod their horses into action and, with their bloodcurdling yells bouncing off the canyon walls, come charging out from their concealment in a headlong dash toward the hapless soldiers.

Liz tried to scream, not as a warning but because of the terror she felt; but all she could do was make muffled grunts behind the rawhide gag. When the Apache let go of her hair, she turned to face him. His mouth was twisted in an evil grin that matched the hellish fire that burned in his bulging eyes.

He grabbed Liz's hair again and with his other hand pointed to the floor of the ravine. Then he laughed, but there was no mirth in it. Horrified, Liz was forced to watch as the mounted Apaches made three passes at the outnumbered soldiers until finally only Hobbs, the black sergeant, remained alive. As the Indians mounted another charge, he dropped his rifle, drew his revolver, and stood firing into the onrushing attackers. Then he clutched at his head, staggered, and slumped to the ground while the Apaches circled the fallen troopers, whooping and hoisting their rifles in the air.

A few of the Indians dismounted and began to strip the blue tunics from some of the dead soldiers. The others continued to circle the bodies on horseback, waving their rifles over their heads and giving out with an occasional shriek. An Apache brave knelt beside Hobbs and peered into his face. Then he motioned excitedly to the others and withdrew a hunting knife from his belt. The yells and screams built to a frightful pitch as the other Indians sensed a kill and urged their companion on. Then suddenly they fell silent. All eyes turned toward the open end of the ravine.

A lone Apache rider approached. He was a stocky, powerful-looking man dressed in breeches, knee-high moccasins, and a loose shirt. A colored headband held strands of long black hair off his flat, broad-nosed, coppery face, and he cradled a Winchester carbine in the bend of one arm.

The Apaches seemed like docile children as he rode into their midst. The newcomer made a motion for the men on the ground to leave the soldiers' clothing and instead retrieve their own dead and get mounted. Then, with little more than a move of his head, he ordered the entire band out of the ravine.

He stayed for a moment, gazing around at the bodies of the soldiers before he dismounted and went to where Hobbs lay. He squatted and looked into the still, black face. From her position on the mesa and in the retreating light, Liz couldn't be sure, but she thought she saw him shaking his head slowly as he reached out and touched Hobbs' forehead. Then, abruptly, he stood up, remounted, and rode into the darkening shadows and was lost from sight.

Chapter Twelve

At first Hobbs couldn't remember where he was. The only thing he was sure of was that he had a headache that made his skull feel like it was going to explode at any minute. He wondered if something had happened to his eyesight, since everything looked hazy, almost black. Then he realized that wherever he was, it was dark. He could hear the night sounds of the desert: the distant bark of a coyote being answered by a chorus of howls; the soft hoot of an owl; a cricket's constant seesawing chirp.

He explored his head with one hand, gingerly, slowly. His fingers felt a line of torn skin at his right temple. It felt sticky, like corn syrup that had started to dry. Hobbs put his fingers to his mouth and tasted the salt of his own blood. Then the images began to return: the Apache attack, the brief skirmish that had cost him his command, and finally the bullet that had creased his skull. He had known he was hit and remembered trying to keep his feet as long as possible before being swallowed by a black, bottomless hole. "Thank the Lord for a hard head," he whispered to the darkness.

As the memories crept back into his consciousness, he began to wonder how come the Apaches had left him alive. But he put the thought out of his mind as he touched his wound again and fingered the crusted blood matted in his hair and over one ear. He ran his tongue across his parched lips. When he tried to stand, the pain was a searing white flash that dropped him to his knees. As he knelt on all fours, waiting for his head to clear, he heard something new. It was the soft nickering of a horse, and, as Hobbs turned in the direction of the sound, he could make out the animal's dark form in the light from the three-quarter moon that was just breaking over the rim of the canyon.

"C'mere, boy. C'mere."

The horse raised his head and turned toward Hobbs. He snorted and pawed the ground before picking his way slowly across the rocky canyon floor to where Hobbs recognized the horse as his own. "Good boy," he said softly, and, despite the pounding in his skull, grasped a stirrup and pulled himself to his feet. He could hardly believe his good fortune when he found his water canteen still lashed to the saddle.

"Thank you, Lord," he whispered as he put the canteen to his lips and questioned himself as to whether he would have strength for the lonely ride back to the fort. He secured the canteen and, holding on to a stirrup for support while he guided the horse, made the rounds of the five bodies that were clearly visible now in the moonlight. He didn't have to examine them closely. He had seen enough dead men to know that these troopers had fought their last battle. What he didn't understand was why they were all still fully clothed. It wasn't like the Apaches not to take at least some uniform parts, just to show off to their friends if nothing else.

Hobbs steered his horse to the area where Levi's men lay sprawled in the pale blue light. A great sadness settled over him, and now the ache in his heart was even greater than the pain from the bullet. He found his corporal facedown a few yards to the front of the other soldiers. Hobbs couldn't be sure, but he wanted to believe that Levi had died the way he was supposed to, leading his men. Holding his horse's reins, he knelt by Levi's side and touched the cold black face, then ran his hand over a head of tight-knit curls. *Thick as a buffalo's hide,* Hobbs thought, and even in his great sadness he smiled, remembering how excited Levi had been the first day he reported for duty with the Ninth Cavalry. He had wanted to be a buffalo soldier ever since he had joined the army soon after the war was over.

A soft noise snapped Hobbs out of his reverie. He looked up to see two coyotes standing about twenty yards off, staring, their eyes gleaming with the reflected light of the moon. He knew he was in no danger from the animals, but it reminded him that he was still confined in a narrow ravine and that there were Apaches nearby, somewhere. Hobbs shook off his melancholy and, working as quickly as he could, undid his blanket roll and wrapped Levi's body in it.

Though rigor mortis had stiffened the corpse, he managed to lash it securely to his horse. Then, grateful that his headache was growing less intense, he checked the fallen soldiers and salvaged what was left of their water supplies before he mounted up; and by the light of the risen moon, a soft blue-white now, he started out of the ravine.

"When's Papa comin' back?" Peg wanted to know.

"Soon as he talks to Captain Horner about someone to take care of Mac," Cindy told her, and she paused to wipe her brow with her apron.

She and Peg were folding blankets and arranging them on a shelf next to the bulk woolen goods. They had spent the several days since the wagon train had arrived at Fort Huachuca helping Aaron update and rearrange the stock at the sutler store. The previous storekeeper had left things in pretty much of a mess, with the merchandise poorly displayed and haphazardly organized, not to mention being covered with layers of dust.

Cindy felt a sudden movement in her womb, and a sharp pain caused her to clutch her belly and suck in a quick breath. She wiped at her face again and held on to the edge of the counter for a moment to keep her balance. Peg frowned, her eyes dark with concern. She dropped her blanket and started toward her mother, but Cindy held up a hand to signify that she was all right.

"Just some pains," she assured her. "They're gone now."

Peg retrieved her blanket and went back to folding. After several minutes she said, "What if no one wants him?"

"No one wants who?" Cindy replied, perplexed by the question. "Oh, you mean Mac."

"Yes," Peg said. "What if no one wants him?"

"Poor Mac. If only he'd try to get along." Cindy took another blanket and began folding it. She found Peg's sudden concern for Mac's welfare surprising and a little humorous. She suppressed a smile as the frown lines on her daughter's face deepened.

"They wouldn't . . ." Peg said hesitantly, avoiding her mother's questioning look. "They wouldn't make him stay with that old Mr. Pike again, would they?"

"My, my," said Cindy, unable to contain a small laugh. "What's this, now?"

Peg's cheeks flushed crimson, and she turned her face toward the shelves behind her. "Nothing. I just . . . I was just wondering . . ."

The front door to the store burst open, and Aaron and

Mac strode in. Aaron's face was a pasty white, as if he had seen a frightening image of some kind. Mac looked pouty and crossed the room to a small cracker barrel and sat down on it, his arms folded across his chest. As she studied Aaron's face, Cindy felt a creeping fear in her breast, and there was more movement and the beginnings of another pain in her belly.

After several seconds Aaron said, "It's Hobbs. That colored sergeant? He just rode in, half-dead. His men have all been . . . He brought his corporal's . . ." He paused and looked quickly from Peg to Mac. "He brought his corporal back with him."

"Liz Pike?" Cindy asked.

"No word."

Mac got up from the barrel, walked to the counter, and stood next to a big roll of brown Kraft wrapping paper. "The Indians probably killed her."

"Now, we don't know that," Aaron said, obviously annoyed with Mac.

"They killed my uncle, didn't they?"

Suddenly Cindy's abdomen was gripped with pain, doubling her over. She clenched her fists and tried to stifle a gasp, then staggered against the counter.

"Mama!" Peg screamed, and she ran to her.

Aaron was at her side in three long strides. "The baby?"

Cindy nodded, grimacing, and clutched tighter at the counter. "I'll—I'll be all right," she gasped between deep breaths, and she let go of the counter to cling to Aaron's arm.

"Sure, you will," Aaron said, and he looked at Mac, who was frozen on the spot. "Find the doctor, quick!"

"Where? Where do I . . . ?"

"Hurry, boy, hurry! The dispensary, next to Captain Horner's place. Tell him he needs to get over here quick. Get goin'!"

Mac broke for the door at a run, pounded across the wooden sidewalk, and disappeared in the direction of the officers' quarters. Aaron lifted Cindy tenderly into his arms and started for the door leading to the back room of the store.

"Get the bed ready, Peg," he said as he walked quickly into the living quarters.

"Is she gonna . . . ? She's gonna be all right, isn't she?" Peg's voice trembled, and her face had lost its color.

"I think so," Aaron said without much confidence. "We'll know better once the doc gets here."

"Stop it, you two," Cindy said weakly. "Of course I'm going to be all right. It's just a little pain, that's all."

"Little pain, my eye," Aaron said as he moved into the bedroom and laid her tenderly on the bed. He put a hand to her forehead, then let his fingers run gently across her cheek. Cindy closed her eyes and took her husband's hand in hers, comforted by its strength and roughness. Suddenly she gripped his fingers with all her might as another sharp pain caused her to cry out.

"Funny ye're the only one left alive, ain't it, Hobbs?" Pike said behind a sarcastic, accusing smile. Hobbs wanted to slap the leer off Pike's skull-like face, but he held his temper, though he could feel the blood begin to pulse stronger under the clean bandage covering the wound on his scalp. He found himself clenching his fists, and his breathing grew rapid.

Hobbs was standing at attention in the company commander's office. Captain Horner sat at his desk, and Loren

Pike was seated nearby. Hobbs was still curious as to why he had been summoned to Horner's office so soon after his return to the fort, but now he had more than a suspicion that Pike had something to do with it.

Hobbs had gone straight to the dispensary when he rode into the fort with Levi's body. A medical aide had summoned the company medical officer right away, and he'd set to work dressing Hobbs' wound as soon as he had given orders for the disposition of Levi's remains. The doctor said that the Apache bullet had creased Hobbs' skull just above his right temple and that the angle had to have been just right for it to have glanced off the bone the way it did. A slightly different trajectory and it would have been a fatal shot.

Hobbs had wanted to ask him if there would be any permanent damage from the wound, but before he had a chance, the aide came back into the surgery and announced that there was some kind of emergency over at the sutler store that required the doctor's immediate attention, and he left on the run. So Hobbs went back to his quarters and had just washed up and changed his uniform when an NCO from Horner's office knocked on the door and told him the captain wanted to see him at once.

"What are you suggesting, Pike?" Captain Horner said.

"I ain't *suggestin'* nothin'," Pike snarled. "I'm sayin' it right out. I think this colored boy here run off and left my wife to them red devils. Not to mention his own men."

Hobbs dove across the captain's desk, sending papers and an inkwell flying. Pike recoiled, knocking his chair backward and struggling to get to his feet, but he couldn't escape Hobbs' outstretched arms. The two men tumbled to the floor.

"Sergeant Hobbs!" Horner shouted.

Hobbs ignored the yell and jerked Pike to his feet with one hand and in the same motion smashed his other fist into his face. Pike went down again, blood leaking from the split in his lip. Captain Horner stepped between the two men and put his hands against Hobbs' chest and forced him back from the desk.

"That's enough, Hobbs!"

Using the chair for support, Pike pulled himself to his feet, wiped at the blood on his mouth, and stood glaring. He pointed at Hobbs with a scrawny finger. "I want that man arrested," he said to Horner between deep gulps of breath. "I demand you press charges against that dirty black nig—"

Hobbs lunged for Pike again, but the captain pushed him aside, thwarting the attack. Pike cowered behind Horner's desk, trembling and holding a bandanna to his lip, which was already swelling and turning purple.

"I said that's enough, Sergeant!" Horner commanded, and he pressed a hand to Hobbs' chest again. "That'll do!"

Hobbs was choked with anger. "No, sir. It won't do. It won't do at all." His head under the bandage began to throb, and he resisted the impulse to knock Captain Horner's hand away, an act he knew would bring the threat of disciplinary action. "Would *it do* if I was white, Cap'n? Would I have to stand here and let him call me names?"

"That's insubordination, Sergeant."

"Call it what ya want, but . . ."

"And as of right now," Horner added, "you're relieved of duty and confined to the post."

Pike gloated, and when he tried to smile, his bruised, misshapen lip twisted grotesquely. He puffed himself up to his full height but kept his eyes glued to Hobbs and moved to make sure the desk was between them. "He deserves a court-martial if ya ask me," he said to the captain.

Horner scowled. "This is military business, Pike. I'll take care of it, thank you."

Hobbs let out a deep breath, unclenched his fists, and forced himself to relax. He knew that any more violence against Pike would only mean more trouble. And he was in enough trouble already. "Sir, what about my transfer?"

"Learn to control that temper, or you'll be transferred, all right—to the territorial prison."

"That's more like it," Pike said, growing braver. "Yuma's just the place for black . . . For cowards like him."

"As I said, Pike, Sergeant Hobbs' conduct is strictly a military affair. In spite of your accusations, there is no reason for me to suspect him of cowardice in the performance of his duty."

"Then how is it he came back here without my wife? And some cock-and-bull story about him bein' the only one left alive. Looks to me like he just run off to save his own skin. And brought one of his darkie soldiers with him just to make it look good."

Hobbs flinched and thought that if Pike said one more word, he would tear him apart, court-martial or no court-martial. Captain Horner gave him a sharp warning glance and moved quickly to take Pike by the arm and guide him toward the door. "That will be all, Mr. Pike. If I need you for anything else, I'll let you know. Good day." Then he closed the door behind him and turned to Hobbs.

"You came dangerously close to getting into some serious trouble today, Sergeant. You're lucky I didn't give you more than just confinement. Perhaps I can find something to keep you occupied until your transfer orders get here."

Chapter Thirteen

Aaron had just come back from the dispensary where he had been talking to the doctor about Cindy's condition. He and Mac were standing toe-to-toe in the middle of the main room of the sutler store. Mac was pouting and had his arms crossed over his chest, while Aaron had his hands on his hips and was leaning forward so they were practically nose-to-nose.

"You just want to get rid of me," Mac said.

"That ain't true."

"Then why do I have to room with that old colored sergeant?"

"Because Mrs. Wry is tryin' to hang on to this baby, and she's too sick to look after *you*. And I'm too busy to do it."

"Then send me back to Boston," Mac demanded.

"You're goin', soon as the relief troop gets here."

"What's wrong with the stage?"

"It ain't due for weeks," Aaron said.

"Then I'll run away."

"I'll help ya pack."

Mac kicked at a keg of nails sitting in front of the main counter and immediately regretted it. He felt a sharp pain in his foot and hobbled over to the cracker barrel. Just as he sat down, a voice said, "Speakin' of packin' . . ."

Mac and Aaron turned toward the front of the store. Hobbs, his head still bandaged, was standing in the doorway, his large frame silhouetted against the coppery sky of late afternoon. He nodded to Aaron and then scowled at Mac. "You all set to go?"

"Yes!" Aaron said, his shoulders sagging.

"No!" said Mac at the same time.

Hobbs came into the store and stood in front of Mac. "Look, kid, I don't like this any more'n you do. But more'n that, I don't like waitin'. So git yer duds, and let's go, or . . ."

"That's all he's got," Aaron said, handing him Mac's jacket. "Just what he had on when ya found him."

Hobbs eyed the jacket closely, then looked at Mac. His expression softened, and when he spoke, his voice was gentler. "And it looks like most of that is wore out."

He steered Mac toward the door, and Aaron followed. "Well," he said, "bring him back sometime, and I'll see if we can find some clothes around here that might fit."

"I'll do that," Hobbs said, and prodding Mac ahead of him, he stepped outside.

Mac shrugged away from Hobbs' touch and glared up at him. "I can walk by myself, thank you."

"Well, then, git walkin'," Hobbs said, and he started toward his quarters.

Mac looked back at the store. Aaron was standing in the doorway, and Mac was surprised at the sad look on his face. He had expected him to look happy, or at least relieved. As Aaron was about to turn away, Peg appeared in the doorway and squeezed next to her father and clung to his arm. Her look was as sad as Aaron's, and Mac felt a wave of melancholy rising in his throat, making it hard for him to swallow. For the first time he realized he would miss the Wry family, especially Peg.

"Hey, kid, c'mon." Hobbs was stopped a few yards away, looking back. "What're ya waitin' for?"

"All right, all right, I'm coming," Mac shot back, forcing a tone of confidence into his voice that he didn't feel. He wiped at his cheeks, not wanting Hobbs to see the tears that had suddenly started down his face. He had to trot in order to keep pace with Hobbs' long strides, and they were soon at the door to his quarters.

Once inside, it took Mac's eyes a moment to adjust to the dim room. What light there was came in through a single small, glassless window hung with a wooden shutter that was only open a crack. In spite of the heat of the day, the room was tolerably cool. "That's your bunk there," Hobbs said, pointing to one of the small, neatly made beds.

Mac looked around the room and found himself conceding a grudging admiration for the neatness of the sparse furnishings. A pair of well-oiled boots stood at the head of Hobbs' bed, and the pieces of uniform and equipment that hung from pegs in the walls were clean and in good repair. Mac walked to a wooden locker at the foot of Hobbs' bunk and sat down.

"Look, kid," Hobbs said, "I know what it's like. My daddy died when I was just about your age."

Mac wasn't interested. He got up and threw his jacket onto the bunk, then walked to the washbasin stand and looked at himself in the sliver of mirror that hung over it. In the reflection he saw Hobbs scowl and pick up the jacket. *What's the matter with him?* Mac wondered, and he turned to face the big black man.

Hobbs threw the jacket at him. "Lesson number one," he

said, and he pointed to an empty peg on the wall. "No clothes on the bunk."

"Now, see here, Hobbs," Mac said, ignoring the sergeant's angry tone, "I've got money—back in Boston, that is. I can make this worth your while. All you have to do—"

"Lesson number two," Hobbs interrupted, his voice growing sterner. "Far's you're concerned, my name is *Mister* Hobbs, or Sergeant. You ain't got no other choices. Understand?"

Mac was hardly paying attention. He was thinking about how he could best take advantage of this situation. "Sure, sure, whatever you say, Hobbs—er—Sergeant. But we both might as well try to make the most out of what is less than an ideal arrangement."

Hobbs shook his head and wrinkled up his face as though he were having trouble with his hearing. He let out a deep breath, then said, "Let's get somethin' straight. I'm only takin' care o' you because I been told to. But I'm gonna do it right because I don't want nothin' messin' up my transfer. Ya got that?"

Mac nodded, then shrugged. "I fail to see what I could have to do with your transfer or whatever you call it, but that suits me fine." He tossed his jacket onto the bunk again. "As I said, I've got money—or will have it soon—so why don't you just act as my valet, and I'll pay you when . . ."

"Hold on," Hobbs said, his voice a harsh, loud whisper. He looked like he was choking, as though he couldn't catch his breath. He put a hand to his head and pressed the wound under the bandage. "That Apache bullet musta done more damage than I thought. I'm hearin' things."

Mac had no idea what Hobbs was talking about and wondered why the sergeant wasn't just listening and paying attention. "I don't require much," he went on. "Just take care of my clothes—when I get new ones, that is—prepare my meals, make my bed, that sort of thing."

He began to stroll around the room, making a casual survey of its contents, taking note again of the neatness and cleanliness of the spartan furnishings. "You seem to do a halfway decent job of keeping things orderly, such as they are."

He was suddenly aware of Hobbs' labored breathing and turned to see his nostrils flaring, his eyes wide and glassy. Mac was afraid for a moment that the man might be ill, or having some kind of a spell, but he put the thought out of his mind and said, "Well, what do you say, Hobbs?"

Hobbs' jaw worked silently, causing the muscles to bulge at his temples. He began to unbutton his tunic, slowly, methodically. And while Mac wondered why he was taking it off now, Hobbs laid the blue jacket on his bunk, taking deliberate care to make sure that every fold was free of wrinkles. Then with an exaggerated calmness he started to unbuckle the wide leather belt at his waist.

Mac was about to remind Hobbs about his rule regarding no clothes on the bed but thought better of it. He felt a sudden twinge of anxiety creep up his spine. It was the same feeling he used to get just before his fights with Fatso back at school. Fatso was bigger, and Mac always knew that he was going to get hurt, even if he was lucky enough to win the fight. And now, as Hobbs began to slap his belt rhythmically into an open palm, Mac had the scary feeling that he might be going to get hurt again.

"Wha . . . ? What are you doing with . . . ? What are you going to do with that?" he said, pointing at the belt. The room was suddenly very still except for the ominous *slap,*

slap, slap. Mac stumbled backward, against the wall of the small room, his eyes searching frantically for an escape route. There was none.

Hobbs' low, raspy voice filled him with dread. "Lesson number three . . ."

Aaron took a stack of clothes off the counter in the sutler store: a couple of shirts, a pair of pants, and two pairs of socks, all used but clean and folded neatly. He handed them to Hobbs.

"This was about all we could find," Aaron said. "The missus washed and patched them up best she could. They may be a mite large."

"Just what he needs," Hobbs replied, and he chuckled softly. "Lord knows he's too big for the britches he's got now."

"Know what ya mean," Aaron conceded. He stood quietly for a moment, feeling wistful but not knowing quite why. "Funny, though," he said finally, "in spite of his uppity ways, he kinda grows on ya."

"So does a boil," Hobbs answered, and both men smiled and nodded knowingly.

"By the way," Aaron said, "where *is* J. Wentworth the third tonight?"

Hobbs gave him a questioning look. "Oh, you mean Mac."

"Yeah," Aaron said. "J. Wentworth McAllister the third."

Hobbs led him to the open door at the front of the store and pointed. In the fading light of early evening Mac was staggering under the weight of a large wooden bucket filled with water. Using both hands, he struggled toward a corral some twenty yards away. A half dozen cavalry ponies crowded around a trough waiting for the fresh water. Mac emptied his bucket through the fence into the trough and stood for a minute wiping his forehead on the dirty sleeve of his shirt.

Aaron chuckled and shook his head, barely able to believe his eyes. "How'd you do it? I couldn't get him to lift a finger. Leastways not without a major fight."

"Somethin' my daddy called hard-way love," Hobbs said softly. Aaron gave him a quizzical look. "And somehow," Hobbs added, "I git the feelin' love's somethin' Mac ain't had much of."

"To hear him tell it," Aaron replied, "his daddy had all the money in the world. Gave him everything he wanted."

Hobbs waited, seeming to let Aaron's words sink in. Then he said, "That ain't the same thing."

The two men exchanged long looks for a moment, each deep in his own thoughts. Then, carrying the clothes, Hobbs stepped out onto the wooden sidewalk in front of the store. He paused for a momentary glance in Mac's direction, then headed toward his quarters.

"Good night, Sergeant," Aaron said quietly in the settling dusk, knowing that Hobbs probably didn't hear him. He turned to go back into the store and nearly bumped into Peg. She was standing just inside the doorway, straining to see into the near darkness as Mac wrestled another bucket of water toward the waiting horses. Aaron could hardly keep from smiling at the forlorn look on his daughter's face. He caressed her hair and put an arm around her shoulders as they watched Mac without speaking.

"Does he get to eat now that he's working, Pa?" Peg finally asked.

"I have a feelin' Sergeant Hobbs'll see he's well fed," he assured her. But Peg didn't look convinced. Her brow wrinkled, and Aaron could read the concern in his daughter's pretty eyes. After a moment he said, "Is there any of that pie left we had for supper?"

Peg's face brightened, lit up by a wide smile. Eyes that looked so sad just seconds before sparkled now. "You mean . . . ?" she said, her voice hopeful. Aaron nodded, and Peg wheeled, dashed into the store, and disappeared through the door to the family living quarters.

Mac poured the last bucketful of water into the trough and stood watching as the remaining two horses dipped their noses into it, then, obviously not thirsty, turned away. "Come on, you dummies," he said. "After I broke my back getting it here, the least you could do is drink it."

"Do you always talk to horses?"

Mac spun around, surprised and a little embarrassed to see Peg standing a few feet away. She was holding something in her hand, but in the darkness he couldn't tell what it was. She came a few steps closer, and now he could see that it was a tin plate bearing a large piece of apple pie. Peg held it out to him.

"Who said I wanted that?" Mac immediately regretted his gruff question; he realized that he hadn't eaten since noon and suddenly felt like he was starving.

"Well, don't eat it, then," Peg said. She turned and started to walk away.

"Wait." Mac struggled to think of an apology—or at least an excuse—for rejecting Peg's offer so quickly. "Ah . . . Well, since you brought it. Went to the trouble. I—I guess I could probably eat it."

Peg stopped and walked slowly back to where Mac was standing. He snatched the plate from her and, holding the pie in one hand, bit off an enormous chunk. He hardly swallowed half of it before he took another huge bite. He had never tasted anything so delicious in all his life.

"I'm sorry you don't like it," Peg said.

Mac took another bite and chewed while he tried to answer. "Your mother—*umf, umf*—is a—*umf*—your mother's—*umf*—a good cook," he said, and he swallowed the last of the pie.

"You shouldn't talk with your mouth full," Peg scolded.

"I know, I'm sorry. I said your mother is a good cook."

"I heard you," Peg said, sounding indignant. "It just so happens that I made that pie." Then her look grew dark, her eyes sad. "Mama's real sick," she said softly.

Mac felt awkward, not sure what to say. He stared into the empty pie plate. "I—I'm sorry," he said at last. "She's not going to . . . ?" He looked up at Peg. "Is she going to get better?"

"Don't be dumb." Peg suddenly sounded very wise. "The doctor says she'll be fine, soon as the baby's born."

"Well, doctors don't always know. They said my father . . ." Mac felt an old, familiar melancholy begin to creep over him. Then it occurred to him that this was the first time he had thought of his father since . . . He couldn't remember the last time. He felt a twinge of guilt.

"What about your father?" Peg asked.

"Forget it." Mac's melancholy deepened, and he was in no mood to talk about his father's death. But as he turned and walked slowly toward the corral, an idea was forming in his mind. He motioned for Peg to follow him.

When they reached the corral, Mac, still holding the pie tin, was deep in thought. Peg sat on a bottom rail, and Mac eased himself down beside her. As soon as his backside touched the rough wood, he bounced up again as though he had just sat on a hot stove. He grimaced and rubbed gently at his tender rear.

Peg was wide-eyed, and her brow wrinkled into a concerned frown. "Did Sergeant Hobbs . . . ?" She paused. "I was standing outside his quarters last night, and I heard him . . . heard you . . ."

"I hate him," Mac spat.

Peg's mouth was a straight line as she nodded sympathetically. Then she whispered, "But Mama says you're not supposed to hate anyone."

"Why do people keep telling me that?" Mac replied harshly. He stared into the pie tin for a moment, then started to grin as the idea that had been forming in his mind took final shape.

"You're a very good cook, Peg," he said in the most complimentary voice he could muster, and he smiled at her. "Can you make other things—you know, other things besides pie? You know, like sandwiches?"

Peg gave him a quizzical look, and when she spoke her tone was suddenly wary. "Of course. Why?" Mac thrust the pie plate back into her hand, took her by the elbow, and steered her quickly toward the lights of the sutler store.

"I need a favor."

Chapter Fourteen

Captain Horner was sitting behind his desk, his brow wrinkled into a frown that almost joined his eyebrows together.

Hobbs had been standing at attention in front of Horner's desk for fifteen minutes, and his back was getting stiff. He was afraid the captain was going to bite the stem off the pipe that was clenched between his teeth. Hobbs was having very little success trying to explain to him how Mac could have snuck out of his quarters in the middle of the night without waking him up. He had tried to make Horner understand that being able to sleep through all kinds of commotion was a trait most soldiers learned early on. Yet when he had to, Hobbs insisted, he could sleep as light as a feather and be wide-awake at the slightest sound. But there had been no need for such vigilance last night, no reason to suspect that Mac would be doing anything unusual.

Horner stewed for a while longer and finally took the pipe out of his mouth. "Why on earth," he growled, "would he pull a trick like this?"

"I guess he just figgered things was so bad, he'd just run away," Hobbs volunteered, and he arched his back to help relieve the ache.

"Nonsense," Horner fumed, "he's only a child."

"Beggin' your pardon, Cap'n, but I seen runaways lots younger'n him."

"Hmm, maybe," Captain Horner said, and he knocked the cold ash out of his pipe against the heel of his boot and ground it into the adobe floor. "Number one, how could he get out of the fort? And where would he go once he did get out?"

"With the Cap'n's permission?" Hobbs said, and he motioned to the chair by the front door. Horner nodded, and Hobbs, grateful for the chance to stretch his legs, walked across the room and picked up the pile of bedsheets that he had brought to the office when he came in to report Mac's absence. Back at the desk he said, "As for *how,* Cap'n . . ." He shook out the sheets to reveal three of them knotted together. "These were hangin' from the barricade at the front of the fort this mornin'. My guess would be that he just waited for the guard to pass on his rounds, then snuck up on the platform, threw the sheets over the wall, and shinnied down.

"As for *where* he was goin', I suspect if he had his druthers, he'd be headed for Boston. But, failin' that, I'd guess he's probably on his way to Benson right now."

"Benson's thirty miles from here," Horner scoffed.

"Respectfully, sir, I reckon he knows that. He's stubborn and spoiled, but he ain't dumb. If I git started now, I can probably pick up his . . ."

"You're still confined to the post, remember?" Horner said gruffly. He frowned again and began to pack fresh tobacco into his pipe.

Hobbs stiffened to attention again, still holding the sheets in his hand. "By your leave, Cap'n, much as I don't like it, sir, that kid's my responsibility."

"I'm afraid you came to that realization a little late, Sergeant."

A twinge of anger mixed with fear replaced the ache that had started again in Hobbs' spine. It wasn't fair; it wasn't his fault Mac had snuck out in the middle of the night. So maybe he should have paid a little more attention to the kid after he warmed his hide with the belt, but who ever thought he would run away? *And if this messes up my transfer . . .* Hobbs didn't want to think about it.

"Yes, sir," he protested, "but with the Apaches off the reservation, he could be in real—"

"You should have thought of that."

"But, Cap'n, there's no tellin' what might . . ."

"You're dismissed, Hobbs." Horner's voice was harsh.

"But, sir, if somethin' happens to him, I . . ."

"I'll handle it, Sergeant!"

Hobbs knew that tone of voice. It meant Horner's decision was final; there was no sense in trying to argue anymore. Whatever was going to be done about Mac would be done without his help. He straightened his shoulders and rendered a crisp salute before he wheeled and strode to the door and out of the office.

Mac shielded his eyes against the fierce glare of the orange-red ball that was rising out of the eastern horizon. The gentle coolness of the night was already melting away, and he knew that the desert would soon be turned into a blistering inferno. He had no idea how far he was from Benson, or how long he would be able to keep walking once the sun climbed higher into the summer sky. The knapsack he had taken from the wall in Hobbs' room, now stuffed with the sandwiches and jar of water that Peg had given him, was already weighing heavy across his shoulders.

All he knew was that he had been walking as fast as he could ever since he left the fort in the early hours of the morning and that he would have to find some shade and a place to rest within the next hour or two, if he could keep going even that long.

As he walked, he thought about the night he fell off the stagecoach, and the next day, how he had wandered in the unbearable heat, not knowing where he was going and not smart enough to seek shade or to rest to conserve his strength. He remembered how he had been nearly out of his mind with thirst and delirious from the lack of food, until at last he collapsed onto the burning desert floor, just barely conscious and sure that he was going to die. And then he was aware of voices, and of strong arms picking him up and carrying him, and . . . Hobbs! The memory of being carried by Hobbs made Mac suddenly warm with anger and resentment, and without thinking he rubbed his still-tender backside.

"I hate him," he said out loud, his voice carrying across the stillness of the desert. But at the same time he was surprised by a twinge of guilt. After all, Hobbs had saved his life. "No matter," he said aloud again, "I still hate him," and he quickened his pace in the direction of a large rock formation looming along a horizon that had already begun to shimmer and grow hazy in the mounting heat.

But no matter how fast he walked, it seemed that the distant rocks hardly got any closer. Then finally, after what Mac could only guess was at least two hours, he approached an area of giant boulders scattered in haphazard formation at the base of a low mesa. He selected the largest boulder he could find, one that looked as though it would afford him the most shade, and slumped to the ground at the base of it, grateful to be off his feet and out of the sun, at least for now.

He opened his knapsack and took out one of Peg's sandwiches. All at once he realized he was ravenous, and the thick slices of homemade bread and baked chicken suddenly became a delicious feast. After he had wolfed down several bites, followed by a long drink of water that was still moderately cool, he paused and leaned back against the boulder to catch his breath. The rock at his back was hard but didn't feel all that uncomfortable, since it hadn't yet started to absorb the day's heat. He let his head rest against the stone pillow, and in an instant his eyelids grew heavy, and the half-eaten sandwich slipped from his hand.

Mac didn't know how long he had slept or what had awakened him. Maybe it was the heat. The sun had moved across the sky so that it was now almost overhead and glared like a fiery, white-hot ball. But there was something else: a stillness—not even the squawk of a cactus wren or the cry of a hawk—and it gave him an eerie feeling that caused the hair to stand up on the back of his neck. And though the sun beat down mercilessly, he shuddered.

To make matters worse, with the sun so high, Mac was no longer able to tell which direction it was moving in, and, disoriented now, he wasn't sure which way he should head to get to Benson. He looked back across the desert in the direction he thought he had come from, but with nothing but a few mesquite bushes and an occasional clump of cholla dotting the flat, barren landscape, he couldn't recognize any landmarks that would let him know for sure.

Mac thought maybe if he climbed the huge boulder he had been resting against he might get a better view of things. As he looked for a possible way up the smooth stone face, he realized that this pile of rock was considerably bigger and higher than he'd first thought. He eventually found a series of cracks and fissures that afforded him some hand- and footholds that seemed to lead to the top. The sun-fired stone burned his fingers, and the razorlike edges along the cracks tore his flesh, but within a few minutes he pulled himself onto the smooth, irregular dome of the giant boulder—and his heart froze in his chest.

Now he understood why the sudden quiet, and why the uneasy feeling that had dogged him since he had awakened. Less than three hundred yards away two mounted men advanced steadily in Mac's direction, moving at an easy pace, their eyes fixed on the ground as though following some invisible trail. Although he was no expert in such matters, he could tell they were Indians; Apaches in all likelihood, based on the bits of description and conversation he had heard from time to time between Aaron and Hobbs.

Both men carried rifles and were dressed in high moccasins and headbands that restrained their long black hair. But what caught Mac's eye, causing his heart to race and his mouth to go dry, were the jackets the men wore, with their gold buttons glinting in the sun. Mac had been around an army post long enough now to recognize pieces of U.S. Cavalry uniforms by sight, and there was only one way those Indians could have gotten their hands on them. For a fleeting moment he could not help but imagine the gruesome fate that must have befallen the original owners of those jackets.

Mac didn't want to think about it. He wanted to run but

didn't know where he would run to or what good it would do, for that matter. Then one of the Indians looked toward the top of the boulder, and Mac knew he had been spotted. In the rapidly closing distance the Apache's piercing dark eyes caught Mac's gaze and held it. The Indian motioned to his companion and pointed, and both men kicked their ponies into a gallop.

Mac tried to move, but it was as though he were frozen to the rock. All he could do was stare, transfixed with fear.

Chapter Fifteen

Scouts comin' in!"

Hobbs ran across the parade square and clambered up the ladder that ran up to the guard tower at one corner of the fort wall.

"Scouts comin' in," the lookout on duty repeated as he pointed to the open desert. Hobbs squinted into the late-afternoon haze and saw two riders approaching. They were Apache scouts, both wearing a mixture of native dress and U.S. Cavalry uniforms. Hobbs let out a big sigh of relief when he saw that Mac was mounted in front of one of the scouts.

He retraced his steps down the ladder and went to the front gate and told one of the nearby guard troopers to open it. While he waited for Mac and the scouts, he tried to sort out his feelings. Hobbs was steaming mad at Mac for trying to run away, an act that could have put his transfer at risk, and still could, for that matter. But at the same time he felt a strange sense of relief that had nothing to do with the transfer. Hobbs found that hard to understand, since he didn't really care whether Mac ran away or not. Or did he? Hobbs had run away once, when he was not much bigger than Mac. But that was different. He had been a slave, and he'd had every reason to run away. But was it really different? Maybe this pesky kid thought he had plenty of reason to

121

run away too. *People all have their own reasons for doing things,* Hobbs thought, *and sometimes those reasons are a lot more alike than we know.*

The scouts came through the gate, and Hobbs held up his hand, motioning for them to stop. The Apaches dismounted, and the one carrying Mac swung him to the ground. Mac looked dusty and tired, but his face was set in a defiant pout, and he glared at Hobbs.

"Where'd ya find him?" Hobbs asked in Apache dialect.

"About fifteen miles," replied the scout who had carried Mac, and he motioned back through the open gate.

Hobbs allowed himself a little smile. He was impressed. He would not have thought Mac could have gone that far by himself so soon, what with the summer heat and all.

"Not bad for a kid," he said to the Apache, in English this time.

"White kid, maybe," the Apache replied, also in English.

Hobbs and the Indians laughed, but Mac's pout grew more fierce, and his glare grew darker than ever. As the Indians waved and led their horses away, Hobbs gripped Mac's shoulder.

"You almost got me into a mess o' trouble, kid."

"Good." Mac shrugged away from Hobbs' grasp.

Hobbs was surprised at the anger in the boy's voice and, without meaning to, responded in kind. "Look, kid, this is as hard on me as it is on you." Mac's eyes snapped, filled with resentment bordering on hatred. "But we're stuck with each other," Hobbs added, "so we might as well try to git along."

"Why?" Mac said. "You don't want me around. Nobody does."

"It ain't a case of whether I want ya or not," Hobbs argued. "It's just that . . ."

"I'll only run away again. You don't own me, you know."

Hobbs stiffened. Mac's words stung with the bite of a lash as memories flooded into his mind; memories of his own words years ago when, as a boy not much older than Mac, he had been dragged clawing and kicking off the Charleston docks and locked in chains for the return trip to his slave master. He stared at Mac for what seemed like a long time and felt the anger of moments before melt slowly into an understanding that bordered on sympathy, even regret. When he spoke, his words were soft, tinged with sadness.

"You're right," he said, speaking slowly, his voice suddenly hoarse, "I don't own ya. No one can never own another human bein'. Never."

Mac's look changed from defiant to quizzical, and he stared into Hobbs' face as though trying to understand what he had just heard. When Hobbs put a hand on his shoulder again, his touch was gentle, and this time Mac didn't withdraw from it. They stood that way for a few seconds, not speaking, locked in a deep, silent gaze.

Then Hobbs turned quickly and walked away, his vision suddenly clouded by tears.

Mac struggled with a large wooden wheelbarrow that was overflowing with hay. The load was almost more than he could handle, and the barrow wobbled precariously, in danger of tipping. As he approached the corral, Hobbs could see the tiny rivers of sweat gleaming in the late-afternoon sun as they ran through the dust and hayseeds plastered to Mac's face.

Hobbs climbed between the rails of the corral and took down the stiff, braided lariat that hung on a nearby post. He shook out the loop and twirled the rope a couple of times to get the kinks out of it. Then he picked out one of the skittish horses milling around the dusty enclosure, tossed his loop, and watched as it settled over the horse's neck.

While he led the animal toward the fence, he stole a glance at Mac just as he lost control of his load and the wheelbarrow toppled. Near tears, and with maddening frustration distorting his face, Mac strained to right the heavy, clumsy barrow and began to gather up the scattered hay. Hobbs allowed himself a private grin and slipped a halter over the horse's head as Mac neared the corral.

"Want to try somethin' else for a while?" he said.

Mac set the wheelbarrow down and wiped at his dirty, sweaty face with his shirtsleeve. "What choice do I have?" he asked, his voice filled with self-pity. "If I don't do what I'm told, I'll probably just get beaten."

Hobbs couldn't conceal a smile at Mac's overly dramatic playacting, an obvious appeal for sympathy. "I just thought ya might like to try your hand at ropin'," he said, his voice friendly and inviting.

Mac eyed him suspiciously for a moment, then picked up the wheelbarrow again but didn't try to move it. "It doesn't look too interesting, thank you."

"Suit yourself." Hobbs turned back to the horse. He slipped his noose off its neck, attached the halter lead to a fence post, and started to walk away.

"Wait! Maybe I could . . . Maybe I'll try it if—if you promise not to make fun of me."

Hobbs turned again. "Make fun?"

Mac had set the wheelbarrow down and was taking tentative steps toward the corral. He stopped, and his look reminded Hobbs of some timid animal's—afraid but eager for affection at the same time. "Well," Mac said, "grown-ups sometimes . . . Well, they sometimes make fun of you when you can't—when you can't do something."

Hobbs began to rewind his rope as Mac climbed into the corral. He curled in the last loop and eyed Mac for a minute, feeling a genuine curiosity. "Why would they do that?"

"They might not mean to, but . . ."

"Do people make fun o' you?"

"Well," Mac started, speaking softly and staring into his hands while he talked, "sometimes my father would get . . . Well, let's just say he got impatient once in a while if I couldn't do things right the first time.

"He didn't mean to, you understand," he added quickly, and Hobbs had the feeling Mac was desperately trying to convince himself of something. "It's just that he was awfully busy and didn't always have time for me if I didn't learn things right away."

Hobbs could hear the anguish behind the words. "There ain't many things we git right on the first try," he said to Mac softly, and he handed him the rope.

"Whether it's ropin' horses . . ."

He took Mac's hands in his own and showed him how to grip the lariat properly. Then he stood for a moment, his big black fingers wrapped gently around the small white ones.

". . . or tryin' to make friends."

Mac looked up quickly, his eyebrows arched in surprise. But Hobbs ignored him and began to twirl the rope over their heads, the loop whispering softly in the warm air. "It'll take ya a while to git the feel of it," Hobbs said as he helped Mac throw the loop into space and let it land with a plop in the dust.

He rewound the rope and steered them toward the knot of milling horses. Guiding Mac's hands, Hobbs helped him throw the loop several times until, much to Mac's glee, a toss finally resulted in the rope settling over a horse's head. Hobbs retrieved it, rewound it again, and held it out. "Here, see what ya can do on yer own."

Mac looked frightened but eager. With his brow furrowed and his mouth set in a straight line, he threw out the loop with determination if not skill; it slid harmlessly off the side of the nearest horse's neck. Over the course of several more tries, Hobbs offered Mac words of encouragement and additional advice on how to hold his hands and how to improve the shape of his loop. With each try, Hobbs felt a swelling satisfaction as he saw Mac's confidence grow, and he found himself grinning broadly in response to Mac's delighted yelps.

Mac rewound the lariat and shook out a good loop. He twirled it over his head smoothly and sent it flying, then watched in amazement as it settled over a horse's neck, coming to rest securely around the animal's shoulders. Hobbs, all smiles, clapped his hands together and actually jumped for joy.

"Yeah!" Mac yelled in a piercing, excited voice.

The horse reared at the sound and broke out of the herd. Mac, still clutching the rope, was yanked off his feet while the horse, eyes wide and nostrils flaring, bolted for the far side of the corral.

"Let go o' the rope!" Hobbs roared, as he saw Mac being dragged across the corral floor. His joy of seconds before turned to icy fear. "Turn him loose!" he yelled again when Mac appeared to be ignoring his orders. He charged after the racing horse and struggling boy, dread of what could happen turning his concern to anger. "Let go o' the rope!" he bellowed again, and he was relieved at last to see the lariat pull free from Mac's hands.

Hobbs was at his side in several long strides. Mac rose to his knees, his face twisted in a grimace of pain and his fists clenched tightly. Hobbs knelt beside him. "You all right? I told ya to let go! Why didn't ya do what I told ya? Ya coulda got killed!"

Mac looked deep into his eyes. Hobbs could sense the hurt, the disappointment, maybe even shame buried behind the tears that had begun to well up. "So?" Mac said, his voice on the verge of cracking. "You wouldn't care."

The words actually hurt Hobbs. "You all right?" he asked again, more gently this time.

Mac nodded, his eyes squeezed tight and tears tracing down his cheeks. His fists were still clenched tight. "Next time," Hobbs said, trying to be as kind as possible, "do what I . . ."

"I knew you'd holler," Mac interrupted, his voice trembling, and he got to his feet. "I knew you'd holler if I didn't do it right," he croaked. And he strode off, leaving Hobbs kneeling in the dirt.

"Wait," Hobbs said, "I just meant . . ." But Mac wasn't listening. He made straight for the trough, where he plunged his arms into the water up to his elbows. Hobbs followed him and stood watching while Mac clenched and unclenched his hands in the horses' drinking water.

"I didn't mean to holler, kid. I was just afraid you might've, you know, got hurt bad."

"Yeah," Mac said, "and that might have interfered with your precious transfer or whatever you call it."

Before Hobbs could reply, Mac pulled his hands out of the water, turned them palms up, and stared. The flesh was already beginning to swell around the ugly red welts where the rope had burned and torn the skin. "How bad are they?"

Hobbs said, and he reached for one of the boy's hands. Mac jerked away and ran to the corral fence.

"Hey, kid!" Hobbs called.

Mac ignored him and awkwardly, without using his hands, squeezed between the rails.

"Hey, kid!" Hobbs said again. "Wait."

But Mac didn't wait. He kept on running, toward Hobbs' quarters, and when he got there, he opened the door gingerly, with difficulty, and disappeared inside.

Hobbs walked slowly back to the horse that moments before had been so frightened. The animal was standing calmly now, the lariat still around its neck and trailing on the ground. Hobbs retrieved the rope and began to rewind it, mechanically, with little thought of what he was doing, while a melancholy that was as deep as the rapidly gathering dusk settled over him. And as the desert night replaced the sun's golden afterglow, he saw the flickering gleam of candlelight coming from the lone window of his quarters.

Hobbs stood leaning on the top rail of the corral, slapping the coiled rope aimlessly against his boot. He stayed that way, listening to the diminishing sounds of the fort settling in for another night, and soon there was nothing but the noise of crickets and the occasional bark of a coyote to break the stillness; and he watched the window until at last he saw the light go out. Hobbs hung the rope over a corral post and, with no one but the horses to hear him, said softly, "You probably wouldn't believe it right now, kid, but it wasn't the transfer I was worried about this time."

Then he started slowly in the direction of his darkened room.

Chapter Sixteen

Mac lay on his back, staring into the dark and trying to decide what he was going to do. He wondered if he should try to run away again. Right now he didn't know if he was mostly sad or angry, or maybe just disappointed and lonely. He had hoped for just a while—for those few joyful minutes in the corral—that perhaps Hobbs was going to be different from other grown-ups. But no, he had to start hollering like all the rest. Mac had even found himself beginning to feel some affection for the big black man—something he hadn't felt for anyone in a long time. Except maybe Peg, but he certainly couldn't tell her that. She was just a girl. It would certainly be nice to have a man to talk to, someone to look up to, to learn from, to—to be like a father. Tears began to well up in Mac's eyes. *Like a father,* he thought, *that you could love and he would—he would love you back.*

The thud of boots on the wooden sidewalk outside interrupted Mac's melancholy reverie. He turned his face to the wall and felt the dampness on the coarse pillow ticking under his head. The door opened softly, and Mac knew that Hobbs was in the room, although he was amazed at how quietly he moved across the floor to his own bunk. He heard the whisper of clothing as Hobbs took off his uniform and hung it up with his usual care.

"I'm sorry about yer hands." The sudden voice out of the darkness startled Mac, and he could hear his heart pounding in the ear that was pressed into the hard pillow.

"I know you ain't sleepin'," Hobbs said after a short pause. "How'd ya like to ride into Benson with me tomorrow?"

Mac rolled to his other side. Hobbs, dressed only in the bottoms of his underwear, was sitting on the edge of his bunk, a huge dark form in a room barely illuminated by dim starlight.

"No," Mac said. "I know when I'm not wanted."

Hobbs hesitated, seemed to be about to say something, but then just eased into his bunk and turned to face the wall. Mac couldn't be sure in the weak light, but he thought Hobbs had looked sad.

Mac was jolted awake by the sound of a bugle playing reveille. Somehow it sounded louder today than it had on previous mornings, or maybe he hadn't been that sound asleep. He had had a fitful night because of his hands, and now that he was fully conscious, they began to pain again and were even beginning to throb.

He heard Hobbs yawn. "Hey, kid, let's go. Time to git up."

Mac pulled the coarse blanket over his head and turned his face to the wall. "Leave me alone," he said, his words muffled. "I want to sleep."

"C'mon, the cap'n is sendin' us into town today. I got to pick up some dispatches at the telegraph office."

Mac felt the blanket suddenly jerked away from him, followed by a gentle slap on the backside. "Let's go," Hobbs said again. "You want to sleep all day? I want to git goin' before it gits too hot."

Mac turned over and scowled at Hobbs. The sergeant

scowled back, but Mac thought his eyes seemed more gentle than usual, his look kinder, and wondered if it was his imagination. "Why do I have to go?" he asked.

"If ya think I'm gonna leave ya here to run away again, ya got another think comin'."

Reluctantly, Mac sat up and let his feet dangle to the rough plank flooring. "I thought you were confined . . . or whatever you call it."

Hobbs pulled on his pants and boots and went to the washstand, where he poured some water into the tin basin. "I'm about all that's left," he said while he splashed water on his face. "Most everyone else is out lookin' for Pike's wife."

Mac stood up and tried to pull on his shirt. Hobbs watched as he fumbled awkwardly with the buttons.

"How's yer hands?"

"Just fine, thank you."

"Lemme take a look." Mac offered no objection while Hobbs examined the welts on his hands and explored them carefully with fingers that were surprisingly gently. Then he went to a small wooden trunk at the foot of his bunk and bent over it, rummaging through its contents. The sight sent a spasm of shivers up Mac's spine. Hobbs' broad back was crisscrossed with a latticework of scars. Mac was repelled by the sight but unable to look away.

"What—what happened to your back?" he said in little more than a whisper.

Hobbs straightened and turned in his direction, holding a small round tin container in his hand. "I was a slave. Sometimes slaves got whipped." He took one of Mac's hands in his own.

Mac grimaced, unable to erase the image from his mind. "That must have hurt," he said.

Hobbs nodded and began to rub salve out of the tin into Mac's palms. It felt cool and soothing, and he looked up into the black face just inches from his own, a face that again seemed unusually kind. Their gazes met, and Mac felt an unexpected hint of affection seep into the resentment he had felt just moments before. But he was still not sure that he could trust Hobbs not to holler at him again, and he recalled the sting of his belt.

"It hurt when you whipped me," he said, a suggestion of his old defiance creeping into his voice.

Hobbs' eyes widened. "That ain't the same thing," he said after a pause.

"Oh? What's different about it? It still hurt."

Hobbs didn't answer, and a quiet fell over the room as he put the lid on the tin of salve and returned it to the trunk.

"May I ask you something?" Mac said, breaking the silence.

"Ask away."

"I know I have to call you Sergeant or Mr. Hobbs, but do you have to call me *kid*? I've got a name too, you know."

Hobbs pondered the question for a moment, and Mac thought he saw the lines around his eyes crinkle and a slight smile play at the corners of his mouth. "Guess I can't argue with that," he said finally. "What would ya like me to call ya?"

"Mac would be just fine, thank you."

"Fair enough, Mac." Hobbs pulled his jacket on over his shirt and began to button it. "You can call me Daniel if ya want." Then suddenly he turned away and began to examine his hands as if he didn't know quite what to do with them; and, with an exaggerated gruffness that brought a smile to Mac's lips, he said, "C'mon, git dressed. We're late already."

Mac watched with envy while Hobbs quickly roped two horses and led them out of the corral. He had almost forgotten about the burns on his hands and was hoping that maybe he could try roping again sometime soon. He studied Hobbs closely as he threw saddles over both mounts and then began to pull the cinch snug around his horse's belly.

Hobbs nodded toward the other horse. "Think ya' can handle yours?"

"Of course," Mac said, and despite some discomfort in his hands, he tried to imitate Hobbs' every move. Getting the straps tight was harder than it looked. He wasn't tall enough to get as much leverage as he needed, but by standing on his tiptoes and straining with all his might, he was feeling fairly satisfied with himself when Hobbs came to inspect his work.

"He's holdin' his breath."

"What?" Mac didn't understand what Hobbs was talking about.

"He's holdin' his breath," Hobbs repeated.

Now Mac realized he meant the horse. "Why would he do that?"

"Ol' Buck here ain't as dumb as he looks. He takes a big gulp of air while you're pullin' up the cinch so it ain't so tight when he lets it out."

"Good for him," Mac said, puzzled again at what Hobbs was telling him.

"Yeah, good fer him but not fer you. First thing ya know, your saddle's hangin' under his belly and you with it." Hobbs gave Buck a sharp swat on the rump, and the horse whinnied and sighed, letting out a big breath.

Now Mac understood. "Gee, thanks," he said, and he smiled up at Hobbs, grateful for his newfound knowledge.

Hobbs finished cinching Mac's horse, and they mounted up. As they moved across the parade square, Hobbs sat loose and easy in the saddle. Mac sat rigid, his back straight, posting in the formal British manner he had been taught in Boston, his backside smacking into the saddle with each bounce. Out of the corner of his eye he saw Hobbs put a hand over his mouth and became aware that he was concealing a wide grin. As they rode, the grin turned into a chuckle, and in a few minutes Hobbs was laughing out loud. Mac felt embarrassed; he knew Hobbs was laughing at him for some reason, but he didn't know what. His budding admiration of a few minutes before turned to a familiar resentment. He glared at the black sergeant.

"There you go, making fun. I fail to see what's so humorous."

"Now don't go gettin' all riled up," Hobbs said as he recovered his composure. "I just couldn't help thinkin' that you seem bound and determined to git a sore backside one way or the other. Why don't ya just set back and try lettin' the horse do the work?" he suggested, and he smiled warmly at Mac.

Mac's embarrassment and resentment faded as he realized that Hobbs was only trying to help, and, doing his best to imitate his casual riding style, he settled back in the saddle and relaxed. He was amazed at how much more comfortable his new position was, and again he felt a budding warmth toward this man he had disliked so vehemently only days before.

As they rode slowly past the officers' quarters, Mac saw Hobbs scowl as he glanced in the direction of one of the doors. Mac followed his gaze just in time to see Loren Pike about to enter Captain Horner's office. Pike turned and glared, first at Hobbs, then at Mac. The look on his face made Mac's flesh crawl. Pike's lips were curled in a hateful sneer, and Mac felt a sense of evil burning in the dark eyes nearly hidden behind eyelids that were mere slits. He reined his horse closer to Hobbs, not sure why but suddenly glad he was at his side.

"I just seen that darkie sergeant ridin' out. How come? I thought he was confined to the fort."

Captain Horner looked up from the stack of reports he was studying. Pike had barged in without knocking and now stood with his hands flat on the captain's desk, his snarling face thrust forward. Horner leaned back in his chair and took his time framing an answer. "I believe you mean Sergeant Hobbs," he said coldly.

"I mean the one that attacked me. How come he's leavin' the fort?"

"I'm not sure that's any of your business, Pike." Captain Horner recovered his pipe from among the papers on his desk and began to load it with fresh tobacco while he enjoyed Pike's mounting frustration. "Now, if there's nothing else . . ."

"What," Pike grumbled, stuttering, "what're you doin' to—what's the holdup in gettin' my wife back?"

Horner lit his pipe and let out a long stream of smoke in Pike's direction. "You know I've got every available man out looking for her."

Pike curled up his nose and coughed. "I got business in

California," he growled. "Every day I spend in this sandpile you call a fort is costin' me money."

"Then I guess you have to decide which is more important—money or your wife." Horner leaned forward in his chair again and motioned toward the door. "Now, if there's nothing else . . ."

Pike fumed for a moment, started to speak, but changed his mind and stalked out of the room.

Mac and Hobbs were about five miles out of Benson on their way back to Fort Huachuca. They were squatting by their horses, studying the ground.

"How do you know Apaches made those tracks?" Mac said.

With a long black finger, Hobbs traced the outline of a faint depression in the ground. "See how soft that hoofprint is in the dirt? If it was made by a pony wearin' shoes, it would be sharper, cleaner. And since Apaches are the only ones around here that don't shoe their horses, ya gotta figure it was an Apache that made them tracks."

Mac smiled. "You make things sound so simple and so sensible. Not like most grown-ups. They usually say things that don't make any sense at all." Hobbs mussed up his hair and smiled back. "Where did you learn all this stuff," Mac went on, "like tracking, and reading smoke and mirror signals, and horses and—and just everything?"

"From my daddy mostly," Hobbs replied, and he chuckled at the admiring look on Mac's face.

"It must be nice to have your father, you know, have him teach you things like that."

Hobbs nodded. "Yeah, I reckon it was. But he learned me about more important things too. Things ya can't see. Like respect for one another. Bein' a man. And doin' what ya know is right, no matter what."

"Even when no one's watching?" Mac sounded surprised.

"The Lord's watchin'," Hobbs said "He's always watchin'."

They stood up and prepared to mount, and out of habit, Hobbs scanned the horizon in all directions. His gaze came to rest on a thin wisp of white rising over a line of low hills to the east. It was hard to tell in the shimmering haze of midday whether it was smoke or just clouds, but Hobbs told himself he had never seen clouds like that. He decided not to mention it to Mac right now.

As they climbed into their saddles, Mac said, "Sergeant—I mean Daniel—do you have any children?"

"I ain't got no family but the army," Hobbs said, and he wondered for a moment at the satisfied smile and pleased look that came over Mac's face.

They rode in silence for a few minutes at an easy canter, and then Mac asked, "Is it fun being a soldier, Daniel?"

Hobbs checked the horizon again before he answered. The wisps of smoke had turned thicker and were broken into soft, billowy clumps. "Some days are better than others," he answered, trying to sound unconcerned.

Mac cast a quick glance in his direction, his face suddenly dark. "Is something wrong?"

"C'mon," Hobbs said, "we'd better get these dispatches back to the fort." And he kicked his horse into a faster gait.

Chapter Seventeen

Hobbs, Captain Horner, and Mac walked out onto the board sidewalk that ran the length of the building that housed the regiment's officers. Horner knocked the ash out of his pipe against a support post and gazed out over the walls of the compound that were darkening in the fading light. Then he turned to Hobbs, his forehead knit in a deep frown.

"You don't think they'd attack the fort? With most of the troop out looking for the Pike woman, that could be a little dicey."

Mac looked worried and glanced from the captain to Hobbs. "Hard to say, Cap'n," Hobbs admitted. "All I know is, that smoke wasn't from no peace pipe. I couldn't quite say for sure, but I suspect it was more of a signal to meet somewhere."

Horner's frown vanished. "By the way, Mrs. Wry had her baby. Another girl."

Hobbs smiled, and he put an arm around Mac's shoulders, and they stepped off the wooden sidewalk. "I suspect that's about the best news we're gonna git all day," Hobbs said, and he saluted Horner before he steered Mac in the direction of their quarters. They went several steps without speaking until Hobbs, glancing at Mac, said, "What're ya lookin' so ornery about? Somethin' in yer craw?"

Mac paused, then said, "Daniel?"

"Yeah?"

"If you had any children, what would you rather have, a boy or a girl?"

Hobbs screwed his face up in an exaggerated frown, as if he were deep in thought. "Hmm. That's a tough one." Mac's look grew more forlorn, and Hobbs couldn't help but laugh out loud. He pulled Mac closer to him, and he began to laugh too.

They continued walking in silence for a moment; then Mac said, "Daniel, could I go see Mrs. Wry's new baby?"

"I don't know, it's a little soon. Besides, it's gittin' late."

"Please? I'll only stay a minute."

"Well, okay. But just for a minute, hear?"

"Thanks, Daniel," Mac said, and he broke into a run and headed toward the sutler store.

"Oh, Mac."

Mac stopped and looked back. "Yes?"

"You sure it's that new baby ye're so eager to see?"

Mac's faced reddened, and he paused for just an instant before he turned and took off again at a run.

Peg and Mac huddled in a corner next to the dry goods section, talking quietly. The soft, flickering light of a kerosene lamp cast their dancing shadows on the wall.

"I think she's sleeping," Peg whispered. "But you—you could wait till she wakes up," she said eagerly. "Mama will have to feed her pretty soon."

Mac was pleased with Peg's invitation, but he had made a promise. "Yes, but I told Daniel I wouldn't stay long."

"Daniel?" Peg's eyebrows rose, wrinkling her forehead. "Oh, you mean Sergeant Hobbs." She gave Mac a quizzical look, then said, "I thought you didn't like him."

Mac squirmed, not sure what to say. "Well, yes. That was before. But he . . . well, he's teaching me a lot. About horses, and following trails, all that kind of thing. And how to read smoke and mirror signals, and . . . I might even join the army when I grow up."

"I thought you wanted to go back to Boston."

"Well, I do. But I can always go back after I'm done being a soldier."

A hint of doubt flashed in Peg's eyes. "So you like him now?"

"Well, yes, in fact."

Peg's penetrating stare made Mac a little uncomfortable, and he wasn't sure why. "Does he like you?" she asked. It sounded almost like a challenge.

Mac hadn't really thought about whether Hobbs liked him or not. "Well, he's never said. But I—I think so. I think he does."

Peg studied him for what seemed like a long time, and a wistful look came over her face. "It must be nice," she said almost dreamily, "when you like someone, and they like you back."

"Well, yes. I guess it is." Mac wasn't sure what Peg was getting at, but she was making him nervous. "I—I'd better go. It's getting late."

"I'm glad you noticed." Aaron strode in from the back room of the store. He scowled at Mac, then pointed an accusing finger at Peg. "How's your ma and that new baby gonna get any rest with you two out here blabbin' away?"

Mac backed toward the front door. "Sorry, Mr. Wry. I didn't mean to wear out my welcome."

Aaron's look softened. "You're welcome anytime, Mac. Just so long as it ain't so late." He put his arm around Peg's shoulders, and they followed Mac as he went out the door and onto the porch. "If ya want to see the new baby, you and Sergeant Hobbs come to supper one of these days."

Mac nodded and stepped off the porch. "Good night, Mr. Wry," he said, and Aaron waved. Mac walked a few more steps, then stopped and turned. Peg was scowling, her mouth turned down in a pout. "Good night, Peg," he said, a little hesitantly. As if by magic Peg's scowl turned into a broad smile, and she waved enthusiastically.

As Mac continued slowly toward his room, he thought about Peg. He wondered how she could be so smiley one minute and look so angry the next. Was it something he said or did? It was almost like she was upset because he'd said he liked Daniel now.

There was no light coming from the window in Hobbs' room, so Mac eased the door open quietly and tiptoed into the dark. Sergeant Hobbs was in bed, lying on his back and snoring softly. Mac got undressed by the pale light from outside and lay down on the wool blanket that covered his bunk. He put his hands behind his head and stared into the blackness of the ceiling.

"Daniel?" he said after a few minutes.

Hobbs' snoring stopped. "Umm—humph—yeah. What . . . ?"

"Daniel, why are girls so hard to understand?"

"You woke me up to ask me that? How do I know?"

"Did you ever, you know, like a girl?"

Hobbs yawned and stretched. Then he lay still for a long time without speaking. Mac was beginning to wonder if he had fallen back to sleep. Then, in a voice just loud enough to hear, he said, "Once. A long time ago."

"I've never heard you talk about it," Mac said.

"There ain't nothin' to talk about. She was Mimbres Apache, over in New Mexico. I found her hidin' in a village the army had just burned out. I was wounded, and we . . . we kinda took care o' each other for a while. I suppose ya might say we kept each other alive."

"Is that how you learned so much about Indians?"

Hobbs rolled over in his bunk, his face toward the wall. "Partly, I guess. I learned to speak a little Apache and learned some o' their ways."

Mac paused for a moment, then said, "Is it fun to like a girl?"

"Take my advice," Hobbs said after another yawn, "stick to horses. Now, git to sleep. Mornin' will be here before ya know it."

Mac wanted to ask more questions about girls, but he couldn't think of anything. At last he said, "Mr. Wry invited us to dinner."

There was no answer. Hobbs was snoring again.

"Indians!"

Hobbs was on his feet before the sound of the guard's warning had faded. He pulled on his pants and boots and grabbed his jacket and hat on his dash to the door. As he raced across the compound, he saw Captain Horner's door burst open, and the commanding officer, his shirttail flying, dashed from his quarters to a ladder that led up to the platform that ran around the inside of the fort wall.

Hobbs clambered up the ladder behind Horner and followed him toward the guard who was pointing excitedly over the wall to the open desert.

"Where?" Horner shouted. "How many?"

"Comin' outa the sun," the guard said, jabbing a finger in

the direction of the fiery ball rising out of the desert rim. "I can't tell for sure how many."

"What do you make of it, Sergeant?" Horner said, as Hobbs joined them.

Hobbs squinted into the red glare at a string of riders moving slowly toward the fort. There was no doubt they were Apaches; probably no more than five, though it was hard to be sure, since they rode in single file, one close behind the other.

"Whatever it is, Cap'n," he said, "they ain't on the attack."

Just then the Indians moved from single file into a line and stopped, strung out side by side. Hobbs had been right; there were five in all. A rider in the middle of the group moved forward and raised his war lance, a white cloth hanging from it. Now they could see that he was holding someone in front of him on his horse: a woman, bound and gagged.

"Hold your fire," Horner said to the guards who had gathered at the fort wall. "Let's see what they want."

"That's Pike's wife," Hobbs said as the rider neared the gate. "And that's Sanchez who's got her!"

"You know that Indian?" the captain said.

"We're acquainted," Hobbs answered, as Sanchez reined and glared up at the men on the wall. Then, in Apache dialect, he asked if anyone spoke his language, and Hobbs told him to go ahead and talk. Sanchez said that an Apache warrior was dead, and that Liz Pike had told him that he had been shot by a white boy who was now at the fort.

While Hobbs was talking to Sanchez, Loren Pike came up the ladder and moved cautiously along the platform toward the knot of soldiers. His eyes went wide when he saw his wife being held in Sanchez's grasp.

"What's he saying?" Captain Horner asked Hobbs when there was a break in the conversation.

"That brave who was shot at the wagon train is dead. Pike's wife told them Mac did it."

"That's right!" Pike said, pushing himself between Hobbs and Captain Horner. "He did! He did!"

Hobbs glared at Pike, then turned at the sound of Sanchez's voice again. Continuing to speak in Apache, the Indian offered to trade Liz Pike for Mac. The idea of it struck fear into Hobbs' heart. He knew what would happen to Mac if he ever fell into the hands of the likes of Sanchez. Hobbs was dumbstruck, unable, unwilling, to translate the Apache demand.

When he didn't speak, Captain Horner said, "Well?"

"He, ah, he said . . . he wants . . . he wants to make a trade."

"What kinda trade?" Pike demanded.

Again Hobbs was tongue-tied; words stuck in his throat.

"Well, Sergeant?" Horner said impatiently.

Hobbs swallowed hard. He couldn't disregard his commanding officer's request for information. "He . . . he'll trade . . ." He took a deep breath. "Her for the boy."

"Well," Pike said, grabbing Captain Horner's arm, "what're ya waitin' for? Do it!"

"Wait, Cap'n, ya can't." Hobbs knocked Pike's hand away from Horner's arm. "Ya can't just trade . . ."

"I gotta get to California, Horner," Pike interrupted. "Don't listen to this black son—"

Hobbs lunged for Pike, but the captain stepped between them, froze Pike with an icy stare, then put a gentle restraining hand on Hobbs' chest. In a calm voice he said, "The troop'll be back in two days. See if you can buy some time."

"You gotta save my wife!" Pike yelled.

"For the love of God, man," Horner answered, "that's what I'm trying to do!" Then he said, "Tell them something, Hobbs—anything."

Hobbs looked down at Sanchez and his captive. Liz Pike's eyes bulged in terror, and the Apache's face was twisted in a hateful sneer. Hobbs spoke to the Indian in his own dialect. "We need to hold a council."

Sanchez shook his war lance at Hobbs. "We will camp here," he growled in Apache. "When the sun rises again tomorrow, we get the boy, or the woman dies." Then he wheeled his pony and galloped back toward his waiting men.

Pike trembled, spittle running from the corners of his mouth. "What'd he say?" he screamed at Hobbs. "Don't just stand there, say somethin'!"

Hobbs fought back the urge to lie, to tell Pike something, anything, that would make it possible for Mac to be saved from this danger. But what?

"Do somethin', Horner," Pike blubbered, grasping at the captain's arm again. Then he glared at Hobbs. "You! You're such a great Indian fighter, do somethin' before they kill her!"

Hobbs maintained his stony silence.

"Sergeant?" Captain Horner said.

"They say we got till sunup tomorrow," Hobbs replied, his voice barely above a whisper.

"Ya mean," Pike blurted, "you're gonna take the word of them filthy Apaches?"

Hobbs couldn't remember when he had felt such loathing for another human. It was all he could do to keep from striking out at Pike. "Their word's a lot better'n some I know," he hissed through clenched teeth, and if looks could kill, Pike would have been dead.

Chapter Eighteen

Cindy Wry stood by the stove in the kitchen in the back room of the sutler store and piled pieces of still-sizzling fried chicken onto a platter and handed it to Mac. Then she picked up the coffeepot and followed him to a well-stocked table, where Aaron and Hobbs eyed the platter with eager anticipation.

"Come on, Peg," Cindy said, "time to eat." Peg put her baby sister in the crib in a corner of the room and came to the table. She took a seat and smiled at Mac, who was sitting across from her, next to Sergeant Hobbs. Cindy sat down opposite Aaron, folded her hands, and looked expectantly at her husband. He put his hands together and bowed his head, and everyone followed suit.

"Dear Lord," Aaron said, "we thank ya for this food, for Mac, and for Sergeant Hobbs. And please, Lord, help Captain Horner get Liz Pike back alive." He cast a quick, worried glance in Mac's direction. "And keep us all safe. Amen."

"Don't be shy," Cindy said to no one in particular. "There's plenty of everything."

Aaron began to pass the food around. With a tiny smile on his lips and a twinkle in his eyes he said to Mac, "Well, I guess you'll be wantin' to get that stage to Denver pretty soon now."

"Actually," Mac replied seriously, "I've given that a great deal of thought lately."

"I bet you can't wait to get back to Boston," Cindy added. Mac wondered why everyone was looking at him so strangely. And he wondered what was so funny, since they were all smiling—except for Peg. She looked as though she was afraid to hear his answer to Cindy's question. "Well," he said, "I've come to the conclusion that Daniel—Sergeant Hobbs— probably needs me to help him around the fort."

"Ya don't say?" Hobbs boomed, a wide smile on his face, and he snuck a quick look at Cindy and Aaron, who were trying to hide their own smiles.

Mac was beginning to feel self-conscious. "That is . . ."

"Well," Hobbs cut in, "I could use the help, but I know how anxious you been to git goin'."

"Oh, that's all right," Mac said quickly. "I'm not in any rush. Really."

Hobbs shook his head and frowned, looking somber. "Gee, I don't know, Mac."

Mac felt a twinge of panic. Hobbs couldn't be rejecting him. Not now. Not after . . . "Please, Daniel—Sergeant."

Hobbs' laughter filled the small room, and he held his arms out. "What would I do without someone to holler at all the time?"

Mac felt a flush of relief mixed with joy and ran to Hobbs, happy to be enfolded in his strong, gentle embrace. He turned and smiled back at the happy faces around the table. Peg's seemed the happiest of all.

Mac and Hobbs stepped out onto the porch of the sutler store, lit by the soft glow from the open doorway where the Wrys stood watching. Hobbs put both hands to his belly. "I might not eat again for a month. Or at least a couple of days."

Cindy smiled broadly. "That wouldn't be a hint, now, would it, Daniel?"

Hobbs smiled back. "It just might be."

"You know you're welcome anytime," Aaron offered.

Hobbs looked at Peg, put an arm around Mac's shoulders, and smiled impishly. "Can I bring a friend?"

Peg squeezed closer to Cindy, embarrassed by Hobbs' question. "It'll be our pleasure," Cindy said, "now that he's learned that helping with supper isn't just women's work."

Amid the quiet laughter Hobbs waved and started toward his quarters. Mac hung back. "Er, ah, I'll be along in a few minutes, Daniel, all right?"

Hobbs nodded and resumed walking while Cindy and Aaron stepped back into the store, leaving Peg on the front stoop. "Don't be long, you two," Cindy said, as she eased the door closed. "It's nearly bedtime."

Mac was glad that Peg had waited outside. He had stayed behind in hopes of talking to her for a few minutes but never expected her parents would go back into the store and leave them alone. Now he stood in the awkward quiet, scraping the toe of his shoe in the dirt.

"Aren't you scared?" Peg said finally.

"Scared of what?" Mac couldn't imagine what she was talking about.

"You know, being traded to the Indians for Mrs. Pike."

"Why should I be scared?" he said confidently. "Daniel would never let them do that."

Peg seemed deep in thought, a pensive look on her pretty face. Then she said, "You really like him, don't you?"

"Daniel?" Mac nodded. "More than anyone."

Peg's look darkened. "More than anyone ever?"

"Well . . . except . . . except maybe one other person."

A tiny, expectant smile lit Peg's face. "Except for my father," Mac said.

Peg's smile turned into a scowl. She wheeled and strode toward the store, where she stopped and turned. "I hate you . . . you . . . J. Wentworth McAllister the third!" Then she went inside and slammed the door.

Mac was stunned by Peg's outburst and let out a huge sigh. "I thought you weren't supposed to hate anyone," he said aloud in the darkness, and he stuffed his hands deep into his pants pockets. Feeling suddenly dejected, he ambled toward Hobbs' quarters, his head down, kicking at the loose dirt underfoot. As he was about to step up onto the wooden sidewalk, he caught a movement in the shadows out of the corner of his eye. Before he could react, the dark form of a man loomed over him, and a yell died in his throat as a rough, calloused hand was clamped over his mouth. He lashed out, kicking and hitting, but was powerless against the thin, muscular arms that held him, and he choked back the panic rising in his chest as he felt a hood being forced down over his head. A drawstring was pulled tightly around his neck and threatened to cut off his breathing.

Finally finding his voice, Mac tried to yell, but with his terrible fear and the binding around his throat, all he could muster was a thin squeak.

"Squeal all ya want, kid," a man's raspy and somehow familiar voice said. "It ain't gonna do ya no good." Then Mac felt himself being lifted off the ground and thrown facedown across the shoulders of a horse, and he heard the man grunt as he mounted the saddle behind him.

Chapter Nineteen

I'm comin' in! I got the boy!"

Now Mac recognized the raspy voice; it belonged to Loren Pike. Only now there was a slight tremble in it, a hint of fear.

And there was a sudden excited murmur of other voices, all speaking at once in a language that Mac didn't understand. Then the voices fell silent, except for one. It sounded angry, threatening, and though he couldn't understand it, Mac felt a renewed fear that rippled along the skin on the back of his neck.

The silence returned, and in a moment Pike said, "I don't speak no Apache." Then Mac felt himself being jerked upright, and rough hands ripped the hood off his head. "But this speaks for itself."

The first thing he saw was the snarling face of an Apache brave, his dark, hate-filled eyes reflecting pinpoints of light from the small fire nearby. A half dozen other Indians formed a tight semicircle behind him. Then he saw Liz Pike. She was bound and gagged, sitting by the fire, her clothes dirty and torn and her eyes bulging in terror. Looking at the Apache, Pike pointed from Mac to his wife. "The boy for the woman."

The Indian pulled Mac from the horse and thrust him roughly into the arms of one of the nearby braves. Then he motioned for Liz, and two of the Indians dragged her from the fire and hoisted her onto the horse in front of Pike. Her look changed from one of terror to a mixture of simple fear and hope. She struggled with her bonds and groaned behind her gag, her eyes pleading to her husband for help.

But Pike just laughed at her discomfort. "Them savages ain't so ignorant after all," he said, and he began to back his horse slowly away from the circle of hostile, threatening faces. "I might just leave ya that way for a spell."

Liz's fearful look turned to one of hatred, as Pike cackled cruelly and finally took the gag from her mouth. "How come you're so brave all of a sudden?" she spat, her voice bitter and sarcastic.

"You can never tell what a man'll do for money," Pike said, and he cautiously wheeled his horse away from the pale, flickering light while he kept a wary eye on the scowling Apaches.

"I don't know who's worse," Liz hissed, "you or the Indians. I can't stand the sight of you!"

Pike cackled again as he kicked his horse into motion and was quickly lost in the deep blackness of the night. The Apache who had made the trade signaled for the others to gather their horses. Then he motioned for one of them to stomp out the fire while he bound Mac's hands in front of him with a leather thong.

Mac was terrified, and he winced in pain as the leather cut into his flesh. As the Apaches were about ready to leave the camp, what looked like a heated discussion broke out. There was a great deal of shouting and arm waving, much of it directed at Mac. He didn't dare think about what might be going to happen to him. His heart froze when the Apache who was clearly in charge grabbed him by the hair and, turning to say something to his companions, drew his hand across Mac's throat in an unmistakable gesture. That brought the discussion to an end, and the Apache leader put Mac up on his horse, climbed up behind him, and, at a gallop, led his band of braves into the night.

"I could charge you with kidnapping, Pike," Captain Horner said from behind his desk. Hobbs watched impatiently as Liz Pike glared at her husband while he fidgeted self-consciously with the bandanna in his hand, then dabbed at his forehead.

"For savin' my own wife?" Pike whined.

"For carrying off the McAllister boy!" Horner barked.

"Cap'n, please," Hobbs said. "There ain't time for this now. Ya gotta let me go after him."

"Don't do it, Horner!" Pike demanded, "That'd be all the excuse them Apaches would need to come back here lookin' for my wife again. Besides, this black coward's the one who run off and left her to them red devils in the first place."

"Coward?" Liz shrieked. "This man fought like a hero. He came close to being killed. Matter of fact, he would have been, if it hadn't been for that Apache who saved him."

"What Apache?" Pike demanded.

"How would I know?" Liz said. "Looked like he must have been a chief of some kind."

"Geronimo?" Captain Horner asked.

Liz shrugged. "I wouldn't have any idea. All I know is, Hobbs looked like he was dead, and this young buck was going to do something bad to him with a knife, when this older Apache ran him off."

"How'd you get to see all this?" Pike said, a suspicious sneer on his face.

"I was gagged, not blindfolded," Liz shot back. "Like I was when you found me, remember? They made me watch."

"Cap'n Horner," Hobbs said again, his voice pleading. "Please let me—"

"I say he's a coward," Pike interrupted, "and I say he should be . . ."

"That's enough, Pike!" Horner got to his feet and turned to Hobbs. "I'm lifting your restriction. When can you leave?"

"I just did," Hobbs answered. He wheeled and strode to the door, then stopped, looking back at Pike. "And you don't wanna be here when I git back."

Hobbs rode at an easy lope into the small clump of mesquite and ironwood trees about a half mile from the fort. He found the spot where the Apaches had held Liz Pike, and he dismounted near the scattered remnants of their campfire and felt the ashes. At least Pike had told the truth about something, but the Apaches had been gone for many hours.

Hobbs had little trouble picking up their trail. He settled into a comfortable gait that would let him cover ground quickly yet enable him to follow the Apaches' tracks with rarely ever having to leave his saddle. As dusk fell and the darkness made tracking impossible, Hobbs rode into a shallow dry wash that was lined with greasewoods and a few mesquites. He chose a spot that he felt sure would afford adequate concealment and where it would be unlikely that anyone would accidentally cross his path. For if Sanchez and his band had passed this way, there could well be other Apaches roaming the area. After securing his horse and feeding him a supper of mesquite beans, he broke out some hardtack and jerky and ate his own quick meal and washed it down with water. Then he spread his blanket and, with his head on his saddle, was soon asleep.

Next morning Hobbs arose with the first light, and by the time the scorching sun was almost directly overhead, the tracks he was following told him that Sanchez's band had been joined by other riders; how many, he could not be sure.

After a brief stop to rest his horse and feed on more hardtack and jerky, he picked up the trail again and pressed on, increasing his pace now that the terrain had become more sandy and the tracks easier to follow. About three hours later he topped a rise in what was now gently rolling hills and gazed down on a narrow valley that took its shape from the dry streambed that meandered through it. The banks of the stream were defined by clumps of mesquite and cottonwood trees interspersed with ocotillo and blue sage, all clinging to life while they awaited the return of the winter rains.

Suddenly Hobbs wheeled his mount and retreated about thirty yards. He dismounted quickly and took a pair of binoculars out of his saddlebag. Then, advancing in a crouch, he returned to the crest of the rise, whipped off his hat as he dropped to his belly, and brought the glasses to bear on the thin wisp of smoke he had seen minutes before. Even with the binoculars, the smoke was barely visible, diffused and broken up as it was by the tree branches it was rising through. Had Hobbs not seen many such Indian fires in the past, he might have missed it altogether. He traced the smoke to its source, a small cook fire partially concealed among clumps of cholla and prickly pear. What looked like as many as a dozen Apaches, maybe more, squatted or stood talking near the fire; others attended to their horses, while still others cleaned their weapons.

Traversing the scene with his glasses, Hobbs saw Sanchez standing apart from the other Apaches, his arms folded across his bare chest and staring at something at the edge of the encampment. Hobbs followed his line of sight. Mac, his hands bound in front of him, lay on the ground in the shade of a creosote bush.

Hobbs watched him for a few seconds, then decided that he was in no immediate danger and didn't seem to have been injured in any way. He squirmed back from the brow of the rise, walked to his horse, and rode slowly back in the direction he had come from. About a half mile later he came to a small stand of trees and reined up. Choosing the most shaded area he could find, he unsaddled his horse and tied him to some brush. Then, using his saddle for a pillow and covering his face with his hat, he lay down to wait.

Hobbs finished cinching up his saddle by the blue light of a three-quarter moon. The chirp of crickets and the occasional hoot of an owl mingled with the squeak of leather as he made some final adjustments, then mounted up. He picked his way as quietly as possible out from among the leafy shadows and headed back in the direction of the rise where he had watched Mac and the Apaches. Dismounting and leaving his horse, he advanced slowly and silently on foot over the last twenty yards to the crest of the rise and again dropped to his belly and peered down at the valley.

The Indian encampment was dark, mostly hidden from the moon's glow by the dense shadows of the trees. The only sounds to reach Hobbs' ears were the ever-present crickets and the distant, lonely howl of a coyote. He retraced his steps, back to his waiting horse, and eased his rifle out of its scabbard. "Stay here, boy," he whispered, while he rubbed the horse's nose. "I'll be back for ya in an hour."

It took him about fifteen minutes to reach the dry stream-bed. He paused in the shadows and listened. Now soft snores were mixed with the night sounds, and where moonlight penetrated the canopy of leaves, he could make out the dim forms of sleeping Apaches, some wrapped in their blankets, others just in their clothes curled up next to the pale-glowing embers of the campfire. Mac was nowhere to be seen.

Staying in the shadows where possible, Hobbs stepped gingerly past one sleeping form after another, pausing to look briefly at each face, making sure it was the face of an Apache and not that of a ten-year-old white boy. Just as he moved beyond the near-dead fire, he sensed, as much as heard, a sound like the whisper of a gentle footfall in the soft sand. He turned in time to hear a grunt and see San-chez, his face grotesque in the moonlight, swing his rifle.

At Fort Huachuca, a troop of mounted cavalry moved slowly through the main gate and into the parade square. Horses and soldiers alike were dusty and tired, the men drooping in their saddles and the horses' heads hanging wearily. A scraggly young lieutenant and a grizzled sergeant dismounted and made their way painfully toward Captain Horner's of-fice.

Once they reported in, Horner updated them on the situation at the fort. "So *that's* why we couldn't find a trace of the Pike woman," the lieutenant said.

"Of course," Captain Horner replied. "While you were scouting south, Sanchez was camped with her a half mile outside our gate."

"But we seen signs of Geronimo, sir," the sergeant volunteered. "We just never got close to him."

"That's not the worst of it," Horner said. "They got the McAllister boy."

"The Apaches?" The lieutenant's eyes widened in surprise. "How?"

"It would take too long to explain. One other thing: Hobbs is out there."

"He broke restriction?" the lieutenant asked.

"I sent him to look for the boy."

The sergeant nodded and smiled knowingly. "If anyone can find the kid, sir, it'd be Hobbs."

Horner frowned. "You may be right, but we can't take that chance. You've got to go after them. And I hate to say this, but right away."

The lieutenant's shoulders sagged. "Captain, the men are saddle sore right up to their eyebrows."

"I'm sorry," Horner said, getting up slowly from his desk. "Draw rations and fresh horses. And, Lieutenant, every minute counts."

Cindy Wry finished nursing her new daughter and returned her to the cradle in a corner of the front room of the sutler store. After she made sure the baby was sleeping, she began to fold blankets and stack them on one of the shelves behind the main counter.

She glanced up at Peg, who was standing at the front window, watching forlornly as the cavalry troop, raising a small trail of dust, headed out the front gate of the fort. Cindy went to her, put both arms around her, and drew her close. They stood that way for a moment, Cindy pressed to Peg's back, both watching the last of the soldiers file out into the desert.

"They'll find him," Cindy said gently.

"Do you think Sergeant Hobbs is with him, Ma?"

"No way to tell." Cindy felt her daughter take in a deep breath and heard a sob catch in her throat.

"I'm scared," Peg whispered, and she wiped at her cheeks. "I don't . . . I don't want anything to happen to him."

"Neither do I, sweetheart," Cindy replied, fighting to hold back tears of her own. "Neither do I."

They both turned as Aaron came into the store from the back room. His face was drawn, and worry lines crinkled his brow. He stood quietly by the main counter for a moment, watching his wife and daughter. Peg went to him, and he patted her cheek and bent to kiss her head.

"Do you think Mac . . . ?" Peg started, then, after a pause, said, "Do you think he's all right?"

"With Sergeant Hobbs out there?" Aaron said, forcing a weak smile. "There's nothing to worry about." He glanced quickly at Cindy, and the sadness in his eyes made her suddenly afraid.

Chapter Twenty

Hobbs felt the bite of the whip as it cracked across his back, interrupting the curses of the slave master. "This'll teach ya to run, ya black devil!" the man said, as the lash whistled through the air again. Hobbs heard the murmur of approval from the small knot of people clustered on the Charleston dock, and he strained at the rawhide thongs that bound his wrists and kept his arms outstretched.

The pain receded, and the vision of the harbor gradually faded as Hobbs opened his eyes and realized he had been dreaming. The murmur of the dockside crowd was now the murmur of several Apache braves huddled around the morning's campfire about fifty feet away. But the leather thongs cutting into his wrists were no dream. He was strung up between two poles, his arms spread wide and his feet barely reaching the ground. He was naked to the waist, and his head throbbed due to the blow from Sanchez's rifle.

Through partially closed eyelids and barely turning his head, Hobbs peered around the Apache camp, beyond the fire to where Sanchez squatted talking to two other Indians. Hobbs turned at the sound of a soft moan, and his eyes widened. About five feet away, Mac lay curled up on the ground, asleep, his hands tied in front of him.

"Mac!" Hobbs whispered. "Psst! Mac, wake up!"

159

Mac stirred, his eyelids heavy with sleep. Then he saw Hobbs. "Daniel!" he exclaimed, "How did . . . ?"

"Shh. Whisper," Hobbs said. "You okay?"

"I guess. But I'm awfully hungry."

"Way things stand," Hobbs told him, "that'll pass for good news."

Mac looked around nervously. "What are they going to do to us?"

"That ain't nothin' ya want to talk about on an empty stomach."

"Can't you do something?" Mac wanted to know.

"I been doin' it. It's called prayin'."

Their conversation was cut short by several excited shouts from the Indians by the fire. They were looking and pointing at the four Apaches making their way on horseback into the far side of the campsite. Geronimo was at their head. The Chiricahua chief acknowledged the warm greetings as his followers thronged around to welcome him—all except Sanchez.

Geronimo dismounted and went to where Sanchez was standing. They eyed each other coldly for a moment, then exchanged a few words that Hobbs couldn't quite make out; but he knew they were arguing.

"What's going on?" Mac wanted to know.

"It may be the Good Lord answerin' back," Hobbs said in response to Mac's quizzical look. "That's Geronimo."

"Is he a friend of yours?"

"Not so you'd notice. But we met a time or two. He's related to that Indian woman I told ya about." Hobbs paused, then added, "He might be just the chance we need."

Mac was about to speak again, but Hobbs signaled for quiet as all sound and motion stopped in the Indian camp.

Every eye was on Geronimo, and he was staring at Hobbs and Mac. Then, with Sanchez no more than a step behind him, he walked slowly toward them and stopped in front of Hobbs. The rest of the Indians, whispering and motioning, crowded around in a tight semicircle but kept a respectful distance from their chief. Only Sanchez pressed close as Geronimo and Hobbs stared deeply into each other's eyes.

"Now, look here, Mr. Geronimo," Mac blurted suddenly, "my name is J. Wentworth McAllister the third. I demand that you let us go at once." Hobbs couldn't believe his ears. He glared at Mac, then looked toward the sky for strength. Geronimo turned his gaze slowly in Mac's direction, his dark eyes cold and threatening. "My father was very rich," Mac continued, his voice beginning to waver under Geronimo's withering glare. "And I can . . . pay you if you'll . . ." As Mac's voice died in a thin squeak, Hobbs knew that Geronimo hadn't understood a word he'd said—and that it wouldn't make any difference if he had.

Geronimo shifted his icy stare to Sanchez. "We do not kill children," he growled in Apache dialect.

"My brother's death must be avenged. It is my tribal right."

Mac glanced from the Apaches to Hobbs. "What are they saying?"

"It's kind of a family matter."

Geronimo turned to Hobbs. "Why does the black man ride with the white soldiers to hunt the Apache?"

Hobbs' voice was firm, and he spoke slowly, choosing the Apache words carefully. "I'm a soldier too. Like you. It has nothing to do with the color of your skin or mine. You must know that. Just ask your sister."

Sanchez thrust his snarling face up to Hobbs. "Enough talk! I say it is time to do what must be done!" Barely turning his head, Geronimo looked slowly from Sanchez to Mac, then back to Sanchez. There was no sign of emotion on his bronze face as he nodded slightly, then turned and walked back toward the campfire.

Sanchez whipped a bone-handled hunting knife from the sheath at his waist and in the same motion grabbed Mac by the hair and jerked him to his feet.

Mac screamed, and Sanchez held the knife to his throat, where the tip, glinting in the morning light, drew a trickle of blood. "Daniel!" Mac yelled, and he thrust out his hands in a futile attempt to push Sanchez away. But in a single swift motion, the Indian slashed downward, his blade barely missing Mac's flesh as it cut through the rawhide that had bound his wrists. Then, still holding him by the hair, Sanchez forced Mac's head backward and slowly waved the long blade back and forth in front of his face, coming closer and closer with each pass.

"Daniel!" Mac yelled again, his eyes wide with fear and dark in a face that was suddenly drained of all its color. "What's he doing, Daniel?"

Hobbs strained at his bonds, twisting and turning, but to no avail. The leather merely cut deeper into his wrists. He barked a single word in Apache. "Wait!"

Sanchez froze, his knife at Mac's throat again, and he glared at Hobbs with hate-filled eyes. By the campfire, Geronimo turned at the sound of Hobbs' voice and slowly began to retrace his steps in his direction. "I claim the warrior's right to challenge for the boy's life," Hobbs said deliberately, once more choosing the Apache words with care.

Sanchez gave a snort of laughter that was devoid of humor, scoffing at the idea. "That is law for Apache," he snarled, as Geronimo reached his side.

"You once boasted you would kill me," Hobbs said. "Maybe you're afraid now."

Sanchez bristled. His eyes glazed over, and his face twisted into an evil mask. "You are not Apache!"

"Only a coward would refuse a warrior's challenge," Hobbs persisted.

Sanchez thrust Mac aside and moved to within inches of Hobbs. "You are not a warrior," he spat in a voice dripping contempt as they stood face-to-face.

Hobbs could feel the warmth of the Indian's rapid breathing and smell his sweat. "I'm a soldier," he fired back defiantly.

"Daniel," Mac said weakly, his voice quavering, "what's going to . . . ?"

"Hush, boy." Hobbs turned his gaze toward Geronimo, who was standing with his arms folded, watching and listening to the exchange of words. The Apache chief stared back, his face revealing nothing. But in that long moment while they stood with gazes locked on each other, Hobbs thought he detected a glimpse of understanding in the dark, piercing eyes. Then, without a word, Geronimo drew the knife at his belt and cut Hobbs free.

Sanchez quivered with rage. "I say he must be killed along with the boy!"

"And I say he has the right to fight for the boy's life."

Aaron stood at the main counter in his store. He watched impatiently while Loren Pike checked the list in his hand, then picked up a sack of flour off the floor and plopped it onto the counter amid the stack of cans and dry goods he had already accumulated.

"That'll do it, Wry. Git this stuff out to my wagon right

away. I'm headin' out as soon as that useless wife of mine shows up."

Aaron felt his anger rising to the point where he could hardly contain it. "This is a cash-and-carry store, Pike," he said coldly. "And *you* do the carryin'."

"Have it your way," Pike replied, as he heaved the sack of flour to his shoulder and began to gather up whatever else he could carry. "I'll send the missus in for the rest," he said as he started for the door, where he paused. "And see she don't forget nothin'," he demanded; then he left the store.

Aaron let out a long, slow breath and unclenched his fists.

At the lieutenant's signal, the troop of soldiers from the fort reined to a halt. The men slouched in their saddles. Some opened their canteens and drank, while others beat at the layer of dust that clung to their once-blue uniforms. The sergeant moved to the head of the column.

"This is hopeless, Lieutenant," he said, as he wiped his neck and face with his bandana. "The trail's ice cold."

"Got any better ideas?"

The sergeant stared blankly and shook his head.

"Then let's keep looking," the lieutenant said, motioning the troop forward again. "And pray we find them in time."

Chapter Twenty-one

Hobbs, still naked to the waist, led Mac toward the small circle of Apaches. As they made their way past the human ring, he could feel the hostility flashing from a dozen pairs of eyes, and an angry, excited murmur began to build. Not far from the ashes of the dead campfire, Sanchez and Geronimo were huddled in a whispered, sober conversation, their backs turned to a stack of war lances and skin shields. Hobbs' jacket, hat, and rifle and side arms lay in a heap next to the Apache weapons. Hobbs took his knife from its scabbard and tucked it into the belt at his waist.

Geronimo turned, and when he saw Hobbs, motioned for him to select a spear and shield from the pile, and nodded permission for Sanchez to do the same. While Hobbs tested and rejected the first couple of lances, an ominous, rhythmic drumbeat started somewhere within the ring of menacing Indian faces. An aging Apache began a monotonous chant, and he moved away from the circle and shuffled around Hobbs and Mac, making threatening motions with a wand of eagle feathers.

Mac's pallid face was drawn tight with fear, and Hobbs could think of nothing he could do or say to dispel that fear. "Will they . . . will they let you go if you win, Daniel?" he said weakly.

"That'll be up to Geronimo," Hobbs answered, as he finally settled on a spear and shield.

"You—you *can* beat him, can't you?" Mac asked in a tentative voice tinged with hope.

"We'll know soon enough." Hobbs led them to where Sanchez was waiting, war lance and shield in hand. Geronimo stood a few feet away, a Winchester rifle cradled in one arm. His broad, coppery face looked troubled.

While Hobbs and Sanchez stared at each other, Mac said, "Does this have to be a, you know, a fight to the . . . ? Does someone have to—to get killed?"

"That's the way it usually works," Hobbs told him, while he adjusted the knife in his belt to a more comfortable position.

Mac was near tears. "Daniel, I don't want you to get . . . I don't want anything to happen to you."

Hobbs tried to smile but knew he was not making it work. "That makes two of us," he said, as he let his gaze run over the circle of chanting, scowling Apaches. "And from the looks of it, I'd say we're the only two."

Geronimo raised his rifle over his head, and the chanting stopped. The silence was frightening, ominous, and though the day was already warm, Hobbs felt a tremor run over his naked torso. Sanchez, his lips curled into a sneer, glared at him, then pushed his way into the widening human circle. Tears spilled down Mac's cheeks, and he clutched at Hobbs, who hugged him quickly, then eased him aside and followed Sanchez into the ring.

An excited murmur arose again from the circled Indians as Sanchez strutted arrogantly around the perimeter of braves, his back to Hobbs. A chorus of surprised yells went up as Hobbs seized the early opportunity and leaped at

Sanchez and struck him a staggering blow to the back of the head with his skin shield. Sanchez dropped to his knees, and the Apaches groaned as one as Hobbs took aim with his lance. In that instant, Sanchez rolled to one side, and Hobbs' thrust went wide by mere inches, and the crowd screamed its approval. Sanchez was on his feet in an instant, his haughty sneer replaced by a deadly grimace and his eyes crazed and burning with hatred. He lunged swiftly, and his lance drew blood from Hobbs' forearm, an action that brought more wild hooting and yelling from the onlookers. Hobbs retaliated, but his thrust was deflected by Sanchez's shield, though it still drew blood from the Apache's arm.

The struggle turned into a seesaw battle, with first one man having the advantage and then the other, stabbing, kicking, stumbling, falling, rising. The crowd cheered every move by Sanchez and groaned when Hobbs responded well, and soon both men were caked with dirt that was mixed with sweat and darkened in places by their own blood.

Within minutes Hobbs was feeling the strain. His muscles ached from the exertion, and his breathing came in deep, labored gasps. Out of the corner of his eye he caught a glimpse of Geronimo, looking on impassively, while Mac stood next to him, fidgeting and gnawing on the knuckles of one hand. The momentary distraction cost him dearly as Sanchez made a vicious lunge that Hobbs was barely able to sidestep and that caused him to stumble badly. He tried to use his lance to help regain his balance, but it shattered under his weight. Amid whoops and screams from the crowd, Sanchez lunged, grinning evilly, his spear aimed at Hobbs' throat. Summoning all his strength, Hobbs rolled away from the attack while he deflected the lethal thrust with his shield. But he felt a searing pain as the point of the spear found the soft muscle of his left shoulder and penetrated to the bone.

Sanchez quickly withdrew his weapon and straddled Hobbs' prostrate body. He raised the lance overhead, prepared for the fatal stroke. Hobbs was helpless, too weak now to defend himself and aware that he was facing the end. But before Sanchez could strike, a shot rang out, silencing the chorus of bloodthirsty screams calling for Hobbs' death. All eyes turned toward the sound. Geronimo, his Winchester pointing skyward, motioned for the fighting to stop. Then he put down the rifle and went to the pile of lances, picked one, and took it to Hobbs.

He turned to Sanchez, who stood waiting, seething with silent rage. "There is no honor in winning an unfair fight," Geronimo said in a stern, commanding voice. Then he walked back to his position beside Mac, folded his arms, and nodded for the fight to continue.

Hobbs struggled to his feet and began to circle Sanchez warily. Still gasping for breath and with his left arm feeling almost useless, he knew he would survive only one more violent exchange, so it had to be his best effort, and it had to be now. With all his remaining strength he lunged at Sanchez with the new lance—and missed badly and fell on his face, his mouth in the dirt. The chilling screams of the circled Apaches filled his ears, and he rolled over in time to see Sanchez throw down his lance and shield and pull the knife from his waist.

In one nimble leap the grinning young Indian was astride Hobbs' chest, one hand locked savagely in his tight, kinky curls and the other hand raised high, with the gleaming blade poised for a deadly plunge. Again a shot silenced the screaming crowd, and the knife, its bone handle splintered, went spinning out of Sanchez's grasp.

Holding his torn and bloody hand, Sanchez rolled away from Hobbs and, his eyes wild and wide, scanned the circle of shocked faces. Hobbs, momentarily relieved, wiped the dirt and sweat from his face and, along with Sanchez, looked for the source of the gunshot. He gasped, and relief turned to fear at the sight of Mac holding Geronimo's rifle, its muzzle pointed directly at the Indian leader's heart.

"Let him go," Mac commanded the stone-faced Apache in a squeaky voice, as he levered another shell into the chamber.

"Mac!" Hobbs yelled, struggling to his feet.

"Tell him I'll shoot if he doesn't let you go," Mac said, his voice growing stronger. He stepped back a couple of paces, his eyes never leaving Geronimo. "Tell him, Daniel!" he repeated, as Sanchez retrieved his knife and started toward Hobbs.

Geronimo gestured for Sanchez to back off. "He already figgered it out," Hobbs said, shifting his gaze quickly from Geronimo to Sanchez, then to Mac again. "Now what're we gonna do?"

Mac kept the rifle leveled at Geronimo's chest. "You're leaving, getting away. I'll keep Mr. Geronimo here until . . ."

"Until what?" Hobbs asked quickly.

"Until you're safe."

"Great. So after I'm safe, then what?"

"Then . . ." Mac started, his voice beginning to waver again. "Well, it doesn't matter. I'm the one they want."

Hobbs started slowly toward Mac and Geronimo. "I didn't rassle around and get all cut up just so I could leave you behind."

Suddenly Sanchez leaped at Hobbs, wrapped a viselike arm around his neck, and pressed the broken, blood-encrusted knife to his throat. The circle of Apaches tightened again, and they began to grumble excitedly. Mac's face showed a new fear, and for the first time the rifle in his hands wavered momentarily from its target.

Geronimo glared at Hobbs. "Tell the boy to put down the weapon. Or you die."

"Daniel!" Mac yelled, fear making his voice thin. "What should I do?"

"Nothin'," Hobbs replied hoarsely, choking in Sanchez's muscular grip. "Just don't pull that trigger! Put the gun down!"

Mac lowered the rifle, holding it in one hand. Geronimo turned and walked slowly into the circle of Indians and stopped in front of Hobbs. Slowly and deliberately, he reached an open hand to Sanchez. "Give me the knife. Release him."

Again an ominous quiet settled over the Apaches. Geronimo's eyes were steely and unwavering as he stared at Sanchez. Then, after what seemed like a long time, Hobbs felt the arm around his neck relax, and carefully, almost delicately, Geronimo took the knife from Sanchez's hand. "Release him," he said again, loud enough for all the Apaches to hear.

Sanchez pushed Hobbs aside and started menacingly toward his chief. Geronimo stood his ground and with a fierce, terrible look stopped the young Apache in his tracks. Then, his eyes filled with scorn, he handed Sanchez the knife, and in the ultimate gesture of contempt, turned his back. Sanchez became rigid with hatred; then he raised the knife as though to strike. A great roar of disapproval arose from the other Apaches, and Sanchez hesitated, momentarily frozen, his face twisted by loathing and indecision. Then he lowered his arm and slunk away to where the horses were kept, mounted one, and raced out of the campsite.

Geronimo walked back to where Mac was standing and held out his hand. Mac's face drained of all color, and his hands trembled. "Daniel," he pleaded, "tell me what to do!"

"Let him have the rifle," Hobbs said calmly, his voice even but firm, "and be careful about it."

Mac hesitated briefly, then did as he was told. The Apache chief accepted the weapon with a solemn look, nodded his head, and cradled the Winchester in the crook of his arm. Then he reached out a hand and touched Mac's shoulder. "You have the courage of an Apache," he said in his native dialect. Then, turning toward Hobbs, he added, "You too, black soldier. You were ready to die for each other."

Mac looked at Hobbs with questioning eyes. "The fight is over," Geronimo went on. He glanced from Hobbs to Mac, then back again and raised a hand as though pronouncing a benediction.

"You are both free to go."

Hobbs wasn't sure he could believe what he had heard. Maybe his Apache wasn't as good as he thought. But he couldn't hold back a smile as Geronimo motioned for Mac to go to his side and nodded his approval. Mac gave Hobbs a quizzical look, his brow wrinkled in confusion. "What did he say?"

"He said this ain't no time for talkin'." Hobbs grasped Mac's arm firmly and dragged him, stumbling, to where he had left his clothes and weapons. With Mac's help he put on his jacket and hat, and carrying his gun belt and rifle, guided them both quickly away from the crowd of scowling Apaches. They came to Geronimo, and Hobbs paused. Their eyes met, and for an instant Hobbs thought he saw the hint of a smile on the broad, coppery face, and then it was gone.

Pushing Mac ahead of him, Hobbs strode quickly out of the Apache encampment and headed toward the low mesa where he had left his horse.

The unrelenting sun beat down on the parched landscape, its white-hot rays reflecting mercilessly off the fine crushed granite that made up the desert floor. Hobbs and Mac had trudged for hours since leaving the Apache camp, and Hobbs had long since given up finding his horse, convinced that the animal had either gone in search of water or simply decided to find his way back to the fort. Mac was growing exhausted, and Hobbs held his hand as they walked, each step a monumental effort.

"I still don't understand why Mr. Geronimo let us go," Mac said, somehow finding new strength.

"I ain't too sure myself," Hobbs answered, grateful for the moment that a little conversation might give them both something besides the heat to think about. "Guess it had somethin' to do with Apache ideas about courage."

"It certainly took courage for Mr. Geronimo to stand up to—what was his name?"

"Sanchez," Hobbs replied as he scanned the horizon in all directions. "You didn't do too bad yourself," he said, and he gave Mac's hand a squeeze. "I guess courage comes in all sizes."

"And colors." Mac grinned, giving Hobbs an admiring look. "You didn't do too badly either."

"Save your breath for walkin'," Hobbs chided gently, embarrassed at the turn in the conversation.

Mac ignored him. "I wonder," he went on, "why the rest of the Apaches didn't make more of a fuss about letting us go."

"They probably figgered you'd talk us to death out here in the desert." Hobbs stopped and took off his hat and wiped at his forehead with the sleeve of his jacket. Then he gazed again out over the shimmering heat waves that had turned the desert into deceptive pools of water.

"Are we going to die, Daniel?" Mac said quietly in a somber voice.

"Someday." Hobbs held a hand to his forehead, shading his eyes.

"I mean now," Mac persisted. "Here."

"Not if that's what I think it is," Hobbs said, and he pointed to a thin wisp of dust hanging lazily in the distance and moving slowly in their direction.

The cavalry troop from the fort moved at a slow walk. Hobbs, with Mac mounted behind him, rode at the head of the column, between the lieutenant and the white sergeant.

"When we found your horse," the sergeant said, "we just backtracked. Figgered we'd eventually find where ya left him. And maybe you too."

"And not a minute too soon," Hobbs said. "We was just about all in."

The sergeant chuckled. "We ain't exactly fresh as daisies ourselves. We been in the saddle for about a week steady."

"Soon as the new troop arrives," the lieutenant said, "maybe we'll all get some rest."

"Them's the most beautiful words I ever heard, Lieutenant," the sergeant said. "Right, Hobbs?"

Hobbs didn't answer. His eyes were closed, and he let his head sag onto his chest and drifted off to sleep.

Chapter Twenty-two

Most of the fort turned out for the arrival of the new troop. The Wrys and Mac stood in a tight cluster on the porch of the sutler store, while Hobbs waited with Captain Horner outside the commanding officer's quarters.

Smart in their fresh blue uniforms, the new soldiers rode proudly through the front gate and formed up in front of the officers' quarters. "I was hopin' they might have some replacements for the Ninth," Hobbs said, as the troopers brought their horses into line.

"Let's wait till we hear what their C.O. has to say," Horner suggested as he took the salute from the new troop commander. Then, while the incoming officer was turning his men over to his second in command, Hobbs and Captain Horner walked out to meet him.

"I'm Captain Walsh," he said, following another exchange of salutes, and he held out his hand.

"I'm Horner. A pleasure to meet you, Captain. This is Sergeant Hobbs, in charge of the Ninth Cavalry scout detachment—what's left of them."

"Oh, you're Hobbs," Walsh said. "Good. I've got some orders for you."

Captain Horner took Walsh by the elbow and motioned toward his office. "We can get to that later. Let's go inside."

He turned to Hobbs and said, "See that Captain Walsh's men are taken care of."

"Let me show you something first," Walsh said, and he led them to the front rank of mounted troopers, to a horse with no rider but with a tarpaulin-covered bundle lashed to its back. Walsh pulled back a corner of the tarpaulin to reveal a man's body, terribly mutilated and barely recognizable as Loren Pike.

"So that's what happened to him," Horner said absently, as though talking to himself.

"You know him?" Walsh asked.

"Guess Sanchez finally got his revenge," Hobbs said before Horner could answer. Captain Walsh gave him a quizzical look. "A personal thing," Hobbs said by way of explanation, and Walsh shrugged and turned away, no longer interested. Captain Horner took his elbow again and started toward his quarters.

"About them orders, Cap'n?" Hobbs asked.

"Later," Horner said without stopping. "See to Pike's body first."

"Yes, sir," Hobbs replied, and as he watched the two officers walk away, he felt a growing sense of dread for what he knew lay ahead of him and what he had to face. And it had nothing to do with the disposal of a dead body.

Hobbs, Aaron, and Cindy sat huddled around one end of the dining room table in the living quarters of the sutler store. Hobbs and Aaron stared gloomily into their coffee mugs while Cindy picked absently at the hem of her apron. Aaron looked up for a moment and glanced toward the crib in the corner where Mac and Peg were playing with the new baby.

"Guess Pike decided he didn't need his wife's money after all," he said quietly.

"What happened to her?" Hobbs asked.

"Just up and left him. So he decided to pull out."

"Speakin' of leavin . . ." Hobbs said, getting up and walking slowly over to Mac and Peg. "Why don't you two set out on the porch for a while? It's a real nice night and . . . and I want to talk over somethin' with Mr. and Mrs. Wry."

Mac gave Hobbs a curious look, and little worry lines appeared at the corners of his eyes. Peg smiled and took Mac's hand and led him toward the door. Hobbs watched them go out, then went back to the table but didn't sit down. He stood looking into his hands, feeling a terrible, unseen weight pressing down on his shoulders.

"Let me get this straight," Aaron said at last. "You mean you *asked* to get sent up north?"

Hobbs picked at his fingers. "It seemed important at the time."

Aaron got a pained look on his face. "Will this be permanent?"

"The army's gittin' ready for a big campaign against the Sioux. No tellin' how long it'll last."

"When are you going to tell Mac?" Cindy asked, her soft voice trembling slightly.

"Tonight."

"He'll be heartbroken," Cindy whispered.

Hobbs nodded and took a deep breath. "I wanted to talk to you two first. Since you're the closest thing he's got to real folks right now, I was thinkin' . . . Well, I was thinkin' maybe you'd be willin' to, you know, look after him. Leastways till I can git back and . . ."

"You know we will," Aaron said.

"We always . . . we always wanted a boy," Cindy said, her eyes glistening. She got up and stood by Aaron, and he put an arm around her waist.

"You couldn't do no better than Mac," Hobbs said, feeling his own eyes grow moist. Cindy and Aaron exchanged sad glances and nodded and held each other tightly for a moment.

Hobbs cleared his throat. "Well," he said hoarsely, "it ain't gonna git no easier standin' here. I suspect I might as well go git it over with." Aaron and Cindy nodded again, and Hobbs, his shoulders sagging and his head on his chest, made the slow, painful walk to the front door.

Outside, Mac and Peg were sitting on the porch steps. Peg smiled a warm greeting, but Mac just frowned, and the look in his eyes reminded Hobbs of a frightened animal.

"Time to go," Hobbs said, surprised by the gruffness in his voice.

"Can't I stay a little longer, Daniel?" Mac pleaded, "It's still early."

"Not tonight, Mac. I need to talk to ya about somethin', and it can't wait."

"Okay," Mac said in a thin, almost frightened voice that caused Hobbs' throat to tighten, making it hard for him to swallow.

Now Peg's smile faded as she looked from Mac to Hobbs, and her face grew sad in the pale light of evening, and she put a hand to her mouth. "Good night, Mac," she said, just barely loud enough to hear.

Mac gave a small wave, then followed Hobbs as he started slowly for his quarters. They walked in silence, and though Hobbs was acutely aware of Mac at his side, he couldn't bear to look at him. After a few steps Mac reached up and took his hand and held it tightly as they walked, in a grip that told Hobbs he knew there was something wrong. Hot tears started on Hobbs' cheeks, and he prayed for strength to do this thing—this thing that would bring him greater pain than anything he had ever done.

Hobbs felt empty, drained, as he stuffed the last of his gear into a canvas bag and snugged up the drawstring. He couldn't bear to look at Mac's face, filled as it was with anguish and hurt, his eyes puffy and ringed with red; but then, he couldn't bear not to look.

"But, Daniel . . ." Mac said, stopped by a catch in his throat.

"There ain't no way ya can go with me," Hobbs said, straining to keep his voice strong while he resisted his own tears, "so there's no sense in talkin' about it anymore."

"Then why can't you stay here?" Mac said, sniffling, and he wiped at his nose with his sleeve.

"I told ya ten times. When a general says he wants ya for his personal scout, the army don't give ya no choices."

"Then I'll join the army and go with you," Mac said, his voice growing more demanding.

"They don't take ten-year-old kids."

"They did in the war," Mac argued.

"They was drummers. Where I'm goin', they don't need drummers." Hobbs put his hat and pistol belt on the wooden locker at the foot of his bunk and began to undress. "Now git ready for bed. I gotta get goin' early in the mornin'."

Mac ran to him, wrapped both arms around his waist, and pressed his head to his chest. He cried out to Hobbs through wracking sobs. "Oh, please, Daniel! Please! Take me with you!"

Hobbs was filled with torment. He clutched Mac to his body. "I can't," he wailed. "Don't ya understand? As much as I want to, I can't." Hobbs' throat ached from his need to cry, and now he could taste the salt of the tears that flowed down his cheeks and into his mouth. "You'll always be with me," he wheezed, his voice cracking, "no matter where I am."

Mac's choking sobs turned to piteous crying. "I love you, Daniel," he said, gasping for breath. "I love you."

"I know, Mac," Hobbs whispered, barely able to speak, and he squeezed his eyes shut while he prayed silently for strength. "I know. I know. I love you too."

In the vanishing shadows of early morning, Mac stood in front of the sutler store with Aaron, Cindy, and Peg, all sad-faced and downcast, and they watched while Hobbs checked his saddle cinch and made sure his bedroll and saddlebags were secure. Mac wondered why he was taking so long but was grateful for anything that would help put off the inevitable.

At last Hobbs turned and walked slowly to the porch. He gripped Aaron's outstretched hand in both of his own and stood for a moment, staring into the storekeeper's friendly eyes. Without speaking, he went to Cindy and Peg, enfolded them in his arms, and stood, eyes closed, basking in the warmth and strength of their embraces as they hugged him back. Then he moved to Mac but was hardly able to look at him, and his dark face and cheerless eyes seemed filled with a pain and sadness that was about to overwhelm him.

"I'll be seein' ya, kid," he said, his voice hoarse.

"My name isn't kid," Mac replied weakly, and he felt tears welling up and burning his eyes.

Hobbs mussed his hair with a gloved hand. "You do what Mr. and Mrs. Wry tells ya now, hear?" Mac nodded solemnly, as the tears began to spill slowly down his cheeks. Hobbs turned his gaze to Peg. "And you make sure he helps with the dishes." She nodded and tried to smile, but her lips trembled, and she pressed both hands tightly to her mouth.

Then Hobbs hugged Mac quickly, not looking at him, and turned abruptly and walked to his horse. He gathered the reins in one hand and stood, head down, while he wiped the other hand over his eyes, then took a deep breath, straightened, and swung up into the saddle. He turned to the sad faces watching him and, eyes glistening, gazed sadly and longingly into Mac's eyes. Then he saluted, wheeled his horse, and spurred him into an easy lope across the parade square toward the main gate.

Aaron moved to Mac's side and put an arm around his shoulders. Fighting to hold back the tears, Mac took Aaron's hand and squeezed it tightly.

"Where's he going, Pa?" Peg said, barely able to control her sniffles.

"Montana," Aaron replied.

"He's going to join the Seventh Cavalry," Mac said proudly, his voice steadier now, and he wiped at his eyes. "General Custer asked for him personally because he knows so much about the Sioux and Chief Crazy Horse.

"Daniel's the best scout in the whole army," Mac added, his voice beginning to waver once more.

"Will we ever see him again, Pa?" Peg asked, pressing close to her father. Mac looked up, eager for the answer; Aaron hugged him and smiled.

"We'll see him again. Someday. The Good Lord willin'."

Mac could no longer hold back the tears, and though he

knew Hobbs couldn't hear him, he said, "Good-bye, Daniel. I love you."

Hobbs stopped at the gate and turned in his saddle. He looked back at the small group huddled together on the porch of the sutler's store and saluted again for the last time.

"Good-bye, kid," he whispered. "Wait for me. I'll be back for ya." Then, with a heavy heart, he rode through the gate and was quickly swallowed up in a desert that was already shimmering in the morning heat.